Jackman

Captain William Jackman's passport photo.

Jackman

The courage of Captain William Jackman,
one of Newfoundland's greatest heroes

by

Eldon Drodge

Jesperson Publishing
2000

Jesperson Publishing
39 James Lane
St. John's, NF
A1E 3H3

Layout: *Jesperson Press*

Cover Picture: *Water Rythms II*
              1987, watercolour, 40" x 26 "
              by Scott Goudie

Canada

We acknowledge the financial support of the Government of Canada
through the Book Publishing Industry Development Program (BDIDP)
for our publishing activities.

Canadian Cataloguing in Publication Data

Drodge, Eldon, 1942-

   Jackman: the courage of Captain William Jackman, one
of Newfoundland's greatest heroes

ISBN 0-921692-95-1

   1. Jackman, William, 1837-1877--Fiction.   2. Sea Clipper
(Ship)--Fiction.   3. Shipwrecks--Newfoundland--Fiction.
I. Title

PS8557.R62J32 2000   C813'.6   C00-901574-4
PR9199.3.D76J32 2000

Dedicated to my grandsons
Daniel, Zachary and Benjamin

Table of Contents

Acknowledgements

I would like to thank

- My wife, Joan, and daughters, Susan and Kelly, for their help, encouragement and support.

- Brian Jackman, great-grandson of Captain William Jackman, who helped me immensely with background information, photographs, and other material. Brian has dedicated much of his life to preserving the history of his famous forebear and the Jackmans of Renews.

- Our Friend, Enid O'Brien, for her help and insight into "life on the Southern Shore."

- Phillippa Dunne, volunteer coordinator of the Captain William Jackman Memorial Museum in Renews.

Prologue

The defroster worked overtime to keep the ice off the windshield as I drove my ten-year-old grandson, Daniel, to a hockey rink in Mobile, a small community on the Southern Shore. The otherwise relaxing forty-minute drive was made all the more enjoyable by the fact that it was the first time in many years that I had driven out this way. As we passed through Witless Bay, I was reminded of the great fishing trips that my father and I had taken to places like Cappahayden and Biscay Bay, further down the shore. I could still remember the experience of being nudged awake at 4:00 a.m. and the long bumpy ride over the then unpaved highway. I found myself searching for some of the old landmarks that had marked our many previous journeys. I kept an eye out for the house where we always bought worms. I couldn't find it. Maybe it had been torn down. Perhaps one of the new modern bungalows that I saw everywhere now rested on the spot where the old house had once stood.

Daniel was not impressed with my running commentary. He was more interested in the hockey game that he was about to play. His Atom "B" all-star team was scheduled to play a team comprising players from some of the twenty or more Southern Shore communities that lie between Bay Bulls and Trepassey at the southernmost tip of the Avalon Peninsula.

As I watched the game, I drank two cups of hot coffee to try to keep myself warm in the bitterly cold rink. Two hours later, victors by a 4–2 margin, Daniel and I were ready for the return trip to

St. John's. As we pulled out of the parking lot, Daniel, thinking as usual about his stomach, asked if we could stop at the Captain's Table, a small restaurant directly across the highway from the arena. Being somewhat hungry myself, I agreed.

While we waited for our food, I read on the flip side of the menu how a man named William Jackman, from the town of Renews, a few miles further south, had almost single-handedly saved the lives of twenty-seven people. By swimming out to their schooner, the *Sea Clipper*[1], which had gone aground on a reef about six hundred feet offshore during a violent fall storm in Labrador, he had been able to bring the passengers and crew to shore one by one on his back.

A few minutes later, as Daniel munched on his French fries and I drank my soup, I glanced at a large poster on the far wall which from a distance, appeared to be a picture of a man climbing out of the sea. Curious, I went for a closer look. The poster turned out to be an enlargement of a postage stamp issued by Canada Post in 1992 in recognition of Jackman's feat of bravery and endurance. The walls of the restaurant contained other memorabilia, including a photograph of Jackman himself, a newspaper clipping from the *Newfoundlander* dated November 29, 1867, and several other pieces of information about Jackman and the rescue operation.

"Wow!" I thought. "This is the kind of stuff you see in the movies or read about in comics. This can't be for real."

My curiosity prompted me to ask the woman who had served us about the story. She assured me that not only was the story true, but that she herself was in fact a descendant of the man on the poster. During the drive home, as Daniel napped, I made a mental note to try to find out more about this obviously heroic figure.

Like most good intentions, however, the matter soon slipped my mind. It wasn't until three years later when Daniel, then in grade eight, brought home a long list of names of famous Newfoundlanders, including such notables as "Joey" Smallwood, Ray Guy and Alex Faulkner, that I heard the name again. Daniel had to select someone from the list for a 500-word essay assignment. When I asked him who he had chosen, he said, "I'm thinking of writing about a guy named William Jackman. He was some kind of hero a long time ago. Besides, all of the other kids will probably pick someone more well-known, and I'd like to write about somebody different."

As I scanned the list, the name William Jackman seemed vaguely familiar. Then I realized that it was the same man we had read about in the restaurant three years earlier. I offered to help Daniel research his subject, and over the next two weeks, whenever we were able to spend time together, we searched for material for the project. Unfortunately there was not a lot of information readily available. Most of the information we obtained was finally found in Joseph R. Smallwood's *Book of Newfoundland*, his later works, the *Encyclopedia of Newfoundland and Labrador*, and *The Angry Seas* by Captain Joseph Prim and Mike McCarthy. A friend of ours from the Southern Shore, who knew a little bit about Jackman, also contributed some information, including an article found in an 1874 clipping from the *Daily News*.

As Daniel had predicted, most other students selected better known personalities for their essays. In fact, out of a total grade eight population of 180, only one other boy had chosen Jackman.

Even though Daniel's project was completed and he had moved on to other assignments, every now and then I would still find myself thinking about Jackman and the incredible feat he had performed a hundred and thirty-six years earlier on a small island off the coast of Labrador. Once again I resolved to find out more about him, vowing that this time I would hold true to my promise.

I reread most of the articles we had used for the project, and found a few leads to other sources of information that we had somehow missed earlier. I tried to recall if I had been taught about Jackman in my school-days. I didn't think so, but maybe I had simply forgotten. Painstakingly, I pieced together the many isolated and sometimes contradictory bits of information that I felt finally portrayed the life and times of this enormous figure from Newfoundland's past. The account that I have now presented is partly factual, based on known, documented information, and partly fictional, interwoven with anecdotes, incidents, and fictitious characters of my own creation. I have tried to take great care not to include anything that would in any way diminish the bravery and heroism of this great man.

The Wreck of the Sea Clipper

When blinding storm gusts fret thy shore,
And wild waves lash thy strand,
Thro' spindrift swirl and tempest roar,
We love thee, wind-swept land.

— "Ode to Newfoundland"
Sir Cavendish Boyle

The *Sea Clipper* was fighting for her life. The small seventy-foot schooner pitched and rolled continuously in the frothing sea. Her vulnerability to the massive waves that pounded her mercilessly was greatly increased by the weight of the 1,200 quintals of heavily salted cod in her hold and the foot and a half of seawater that she had taken on.

Her deck had been swept clean. The first of the three twenty-foot waves that hit her in rapid succession had wrenched two of her four dories from their davits and sent them spinning away into the distance. Before the men could secure the other dories, they too were carried away when the next wave raked the vessel's deck from bow to stern. The skiff that was towed behind had also been lost just minutes earlier when its tow line had snapped like a piece of thread. The third and largest wave had smashed the forecastle housing, ripping away all but one small section that now leaned sharply toward the starboard side of the vessel.

The schooner's skipper, Albert Rideout, and the other men on deck held fast to the lifeline that they had rigged fore and aft as they moved about the vessel lest they too be washed overboard. The sixty-seven-year-old Rideout found it hard going. The rheumatism in his lower back and legs made each step on the slippery, constantly shifting deck a painful challenge. Compensating for his inability to move as nimbly as most of the other men, he pulled himself along mainly with the strength of his arms and shoulders, exhausted from his exertions. Despite his heavy clothing, he, like the other men on deck, was soaked to the skin by the driving rain and snow. Yet his senses were acutely tuned to the situation that they were in and he knew that he would have to call on his fifty-four years' experience on the sea to see his schooner and her crew safely through the tempest that confronted them.

Before Albert left home the previous June he had promised his wife Margaret that this would be his last voyage to Labrador. He would stay closer to home and fish the waters of Conception Bay, perhaps even give up fishing altogether. Despite the chaotic activity of the moment, he was suddenly able to visualize Margaret's face, and hoped that he would live through this to be able to keep his promise to her.

As he tried to see through the blinding snow squall, Rideout prayed that the anchor holding the schooner to the shallow bottom of Indian Tickle would hold fast. He wasn't yet aware that the terrible strain had already opened a large seam in her bow through which the sea now poured in at an alarming rate.

Aaron Bartlett, the man at his side, shouted to make himself heard above the roar of the wind. His voice and the relative calm of his words belied the fear that burned like a hot poker in the pit of his stomach. He too, like Rideout, was a veteran of many years at sea and was fully cognizant of the peril that they were now facing.

"Skipper, what do ye think? Will she stay?"

Eyeing a section of sail that still slapped uselessly in the wind, the skipper took a few seconds before answering, "Aaron, b'y, I don't know. I just don't know. I don't think I ever seen it as bad as this before. If she don't hold, then I s'pose we'll be beat up on the rocks for sure."

Of even greater concern to Rideout was the severe listing of the schooner as she strained on her leash. He knew that she was dangerously close to capsizing. He finally made the decision with which he had been struggling for several minutes. Over the roar of the wind, he gave the order to his men to cut away the schooner's spars.

"B'ys, get the axes. They got to come down. We got no choice. That's our only chance now. The sea is getting worse by the minute. Hurry now, b'ys, while we still got the chance."

The axes had scarcely taken their first bite when Rideout and the others suddenly realized that their schooner was no longer at anchor. She was adrift. Unable to withstand the enormous strain, her chain had parted. Propelled by the hurricane-force wind and the mountainous waves, the *Sea Clipper* and her crew now drifted out of control, picking up speed and momentum as they moved toward the rocks and reefs that the men knew lay ahead. In her damaged and overburdened condition, she was unable to respond to the directions of the man at the helm.

Below deck, the other members of the schooner's ten-man crew pumped feverishly to try to keep ahead of the water that cascaded in relentlessly each time the schooner buried her nose in the sea. The knee-high water they stood in told them that they were fighting a losing battle. Experienced seamen all, they had trouble maintaining their balance as the schooner pitched and bucked with every wave that struck her.

Simon Ryan, the oldest of them all, retched uncontrollably. The stench of his vomit mingled with the smell of the salt bulk and the sweat of the men, making the close confines of the hold almost unbearable. Ned Sturge, twelve years old and making his first voyage, struggled hard to mask his own fear. He too was sick, trying desperately to fight down the nausea and panic that welled up inside him. He felt claustrophobic and had difficulty breathing. He wondered if he would ever see his mother and his family again. Although he was not alone in the hold, he felt extremely lonely and sad.

Every time the vessel climbed to the crest of a new wave and began its plunge into the long trough that followed, each man in the hold held his breath, counting the seconds until the schooner finally arrested its fall and began to rise again. Each descent seemed like it would never end. They all knew that the next time the ship, with her great load of fish and seawater, might continue to plummet downward without ever rising again, taking them to a deep and watery grave.

Two days earlier the *Sea Clipper* and her crew had begun their five-hundred-mile journey home to Conception Bay. Sailing leisurely southward through Indian Tickle, an expanse of water southeast of the entrance to Groswater Bay on the Labrador coast, they stopped occasionally to retry some of the places that had yielded good results on their trip north several weeks earlier. At 6:00 a.m. they were fishing peacefully about three miles offshore with the schooner's dories deployed in two-man teams working handlines. The large quantity of cod stored in the hold already made this voyage more successful than most. Another day or two should have seen the vessel loaded to full capacity.

The fresh breeze of the morning deteriorated into strong, sometimes violent gusts from the north-east and dark ominous clouds began to cover the horizon. Skipper Albert Rideout winched in the anchor, gathered in his men and dories, and head-ed for the nearest safe haven, Spotted Island Harbour, three or four miles away. His instinct and years of experience on the salt water told him that bad weather was in store. The *Sea Clipper*, with her bumper load, rode at least a foot and a half lower in the water than usual. Rideout knew that in this condition, his vessel would be at great risk in a heavy sea.

The wind suddenly shifted from the north-west, and the weather intensified perceptibly by the minute. Rideout and his crew were by now extremely anxious to reach the safety of their destination. Then, almost without warning, the men of the *Sea Clipper* suddenly found themselves in the midst of one of the worst fall storms ever recorded on the coast of Labrador. The October Gale of 1867 would, before it was done, claim forty-two ships and the lives of forty people. This was eclipsed only by the Great Gale of 1885 which took almost a hundred ships, the lives of three hundred men, women and children and left hundreds of others homeless and destitute.

To proceed under full sail in the weather that had by now degenerated into a full fledged hurricane was certain suicide. Rideout did the only other thing possible in the circumstances. He dropped anchor to attempt to ride out the storm. He reckoned that he was still about a mile and a half north-west of the north shore of Spotted Island.

Unknown to Skipper Rideout and his men, another vessel, the *Loon*[2], was at anchor less than an eighth of a mile to the windward of them. Like the *Sea Clipper*, she too was desperately trying to ride out the storm.

Slightly smaller than the *Sea Clipper*, the *Loon* was another Conception Bay fishing schooner. On this day, however, she was not carrying fish. Her cargo was a human one. Earlier that morning she had picked up fifteen men and women who had spent the season in migratory summer fishing outposts along the coast of Labrador and was ferrying them to Spotted Island. There they would board the vessels to take them back to their homes in Harbour Grace, Carbonear, Bay Roberts, and other Conception Bay communities.

The *Loon*, light and as yet undamaged, was not in quite the same dire predicament as the *Sea Clipper*. Nevertheless, her skipper, Simon Dawe, was worried. Unable to see more than a schooner-length ahead, he knew that if their anchor didn't hold they would be in grave peril. Most of the passengers waited below, preferring the stale air and the constant buffeting of the vessel to the discomfort of the elements raging above. The handful who remained on deck peered constantly into the driving wind and snow. Among those on deck was one woman. Although she was frail and getting along in years, Elizabeth Stringer was determined to face whatever confronted her head-on. That was the way she had lived her entire life. Known to almost everyone as Aunt Liza, she had been coming to Labrador every summer since she was a young girl, working mostly as a cook and helping out in many other ways. After her husband had died five years earlier, she had continued to make these annual northward voyages simply because it was the life to which she was accustomed and she had no desire to change it. Over the years, Elizabeth had seen and experienced many strange and wonderful things in this great northland, and the terrible storm that she now found herself in caused her no great fear or distress.

The *Loon* was straining on her chain when one of the passengers suddenly pointed and cried, "My God! Look!" In disbelief, the others saw, looming out of the storm like a spectral apparition, the *Sea Clipper*, bearing down on them from a distance of less than fifty yards.

Aboard the *Sea Clipper*, Albert Rideout saw the other schooner too late to take the evasive action that would have avoided the now inevitable collision. In any event, his frantic efforts to swing the bow of the *Sea Clipper* around were ignored by a vessel too overloaded with fish and tons of shifting sea water. As the crew and passengers on the two converging vessels stared in trepidation at each other across the short expanse of water, the distance between the two schooners rapidly closed to thirty yards, then twenty.

Simon Ryan, young Ned Sturge, and the other men below deck on the *Sea Clipper* were unaware of the scene unfolding above them until they were violently knocked off their feet and dashed against the walls of the ship and into each other. The impact of the collision left them dazed and terrified. They clambered up to the deck, certain that the catastrophe that they had been dreading for the past hour was finally upon them. They stared in disbelief at the spectacle of the *Loon* impaled on the bow of the *Sea Clipper* and were not prepared for the incredible sight of men and women scrambling like spiders to flee from their own stricken ship.

Simon Dawe, with the quickness of mind that had kept him alive during his forty-one years at sea, knew immediately that his vessel was doomed. With almost reflex action, the *Loon's* skipper managed to cast a line to the *Sea Clipper* where it was seized and secured to the forward mast. He knew that they had only a few minutes at the most. He bullied, coaxed and cajoled the seventeen passengers and crewmen in his charge one by one across the tangled mass of splintered wood, rope, and canvas where the two schooners were now joined. The short span of ten feet was probably the most perilous journey many of these men and women would ever take. One false step meant certain death, either by drowning in the churning sea below or crushed between the grating walls of the vessels. They all had to carefully pick their way through the debris, and synchronize their jump onto the deck of the *Sea Clipper* with the crashing of the waves against the two joined vessels. Outstretched arms were waiting to catch them. Several of them would have fallen into the sea had they not been grabbed before they dropped into the void that suddenly opened between the two schooners. Many received cuts, bruises, and other injuries in their jump to safety.

Coupled beam to bow, the two schooners drifted behind the headland that Captain Rideout recognized as Black Head. The handful of people still left on the *Loon* fought furiously to gain the relative safety of the *Sea Clipper*. Now sheltered slightly from the full fury of the wind, the vessels, still locked together in a deadly embrace, continued to sidle toward the small rocky cove that lay a quarter of a mile ahead. Despite being in the lee of the land, the waves, now longer because of the shallower water, were no less treacherous than they had been in the open sea. When the last man from the *Loon* set foot on the *Sea Clipper's* deck, Captain Dawe prepared to come across himself. Almost at the same instant that he started forward, the two vessels were wrenched apart by the fury of the waves, and Dawe was hurled into the foaming seas. Incredibly, he held onto the rope that still somehow remained fastened to the *Sea Clipper's* mast. With great effort, he was pulled from the sea. Exhausted, but relatively unhurt, he was soon again on his feet. His indomitable spirit and concern for the others would not permit his wet and tired body to take the rest that it craved. More than anything else he was bothered by the fact that he had lost one of his boots in the process.

They all watched in silence as the *Loon*, with a great gaping hole in her side, settled stern-first in the water. With her bowsprit pointing almost straight upwards, she disappeared from sight in less than three minutes.

Exhausted but thankful for their deliverance from the collision, the twenty-seven men and women were unaware of the new and even greater danger that lurked a few short feet beneath them. Captain Rideout, scanning the cove ahead, trying to gauge where they would land, hoped that the *Sea Clipper* would run aground close to shore before striking the rocks that lined the cove's edge. He was the first one to recognize the shudder that went through the schooner when she hit the line of jagged rocks rising from the reef directly below her keel. The next wave pushed her further onto the sharp rocks, sending all hands reeling. Within seconds, the *Sea Clipper* was driven firmly upon the reef, its bottom ripped open from stem to stern. Heeled over sharply in the direction of the cove, the schooner now bore the full brunt of the pounding sea against her exposed hull. The men and women clung tenaciously to anything within reach that would prevent them from being flung into the angry water.

The shore stood a tantalizing six hundred feet away. Snatched from disaster only minutes earlier, the twenty-seven souls on the doomed *Sea Clipper* suddenly found themselves again on the brink of certain death.

One of the great ironies of the Newfoundland fishery is that very few fishermen, despite spending their entire lives on the water, know how to swim. Even the two or three men on board who could do so were reluctant to attempt the perilous swim to shore.

Captain Rideout, lamenting the earlier loss of his dories, remembered the sealing gun that he always kept in the forecastle. Leaving the relative stability of the railing, he carefully crawled back to retrieve it. Even though he realized that it would be nearly impossible for anyone to hear the old musket in the howling wind, he nevertheless managed to fire off a few volleys before its ancient mechanism overheated and jammed.

Thus the men and women of the ill-fated *Sea Clipper* awaited their destiny, truly believing that they could expect no salvation in this cold, lonely, God-forsaken place.

Model of the Sea Clipper *in distress*.
Photo taken at Captain's Table Restaurant, Mobile,
owned by Arthur Jackman, great grandson of Captain William Jackman.

With the Permission of the J.R. Smallwood Centre for Newfoundland Studies.

Spotted Island, Labrador, where Jackman's famous rescue of the passengers and crew of the Sea Clipper took place. Circa 1900.

Born in Renews

COME ALL YOU GOOD PEOPLE, I'LL SING YOU A SONG
ABOUT THE POOR PEOPLE HOW THEY GET ALONG;
THEY'LL START IN THE SPRING, FINISH UP IN THE FALL,
AND WHEN IT'S ALL OVER THEY HAVE NOTHING AT ALL,
AND IT'S HARD, HARD TIMES.

— "Hard, Hard Times"
Author unknown

Thirty years earlier, on May 20, 1837, the man who would play an epic role in the events that ensued on Spotted Island was born in the village of Renews on the Southern Shore of Newfoundland. The "shore" is generally thought of as the stretch of coastline on the Avalon Peninsula that lies between Bay Bulls in the north and Cape Race in the south. Some view it as extending a few miles further south to encompass the Bay of Trepassey on the peninsula's southernmost tip. The deep, fiord-like indentations of the coast, the boggy, barren and rock-filled terrain, and the lack of significant forestation are evidence of the massive glaciers that moved over the region millions of years earlier.

As community names like Fermeuse, La Manche and Aquaforte suggest, many of the shore's towns and villages were originally settled by the migratory Portuguese and French fishermen who exploited the rich fishing grounds of the Southern Shore as early as the end of the fifteenth century. By the mid-

1700's, however, any trace of the early Portuguese and French influence in the area had all but disappeared, and the shore was predominantly Irish and almost entirely Roman Catholic.

In the early and mid-1800's, the combined populations of the twenty or more communities that lay within the roughly defined boundaries of the Southern Shore probably never exceeded three thousand. What little wealth existed in the region was concentrated in the larger towns of Bay Bulls, Witless Bay and Ferryland.

Almost totally dependent on the cod fishery for survival, many families during this time period lived their entire lives in poverty. Particularly vulnerable to starvation, hardship, and deprivation were smaller communities like Mobile, Tors Cove, and Brigus South, whose people subsisted from year to year at the whim of the wealthy fishing and sealing merchants in St. John's. Every fall or spring, even in their best years, many of the fishermen and sealers of the Southern Shore received barely enough compensation for their catches to enable them to extend their credit with the merchants for another winter. In poorer seasons, men and their families were often left in dire straits to face a winter of extreme hunger and hardship.

While there are very few recorded instances of actual starvation in Newfoundland's history, thousands of men, women, and children died long before their time, their bodies gaunt and wasted by years of malnutrition and deprivation. Many rarely knew in their lifetime the jingle of a few coins in their pockets. One well-known sealing master was once known to have paid his sealers their paltry share of the voyage's profits before they left the vessel, only to collect it back from them minutes later on the wharf as payment owing to him for the credit he had previously extended to them.

Since the arrival of the first ships from Portugal and France at the turn of the sixteenth century, the vast majority of the fishermen of the Southern Shore had exploited the inshore cod fishery in small boats. Unlike their counterparts in Conception Bay, Trinity Bay, and Bonavista Bay, who pursued the Banks fishery in large schooners or made long voyages to the waters of coastal Labrador, they didn't have to venture beyond the rich fishing grounds on their own doorstep. It wasn't until the mid-1800's when they began to supplement their meagre incomes by participating in the fledgling seal fishery conducted off the coast of northern Newfoundland each spring that many of these fishermen left the confines of the shore for the first time.

Despite their hardships, the people of the Southern Shore remained true to their religious beliefs. Their faith helped them face the tribulations of daily living. The early influence of the Roman Catholic Church was still very much in evidence in 1949, the first year of Newfoundland's union with Canada. At that time the Honourable Joseph R. Smallwood almost single-handedly engineered Newfoundland's entry into Confederation, and then became the province's first Premier. Mr. Smallwood attempted to blackmail the residents of the Southern Shore into electing his Liberal candidate, Gregory Power, by threatening to withhold development projects and government services. The voters of the Ferryland electoral district, however, were not intimidated by Smallwood's tactics and instead followed the urging of the Church and voted overwhelmingly for the opposing Progressive Conservative Party.

The community of Renews is situated about fifteen miles south of Ferryland, the Southern Shore's "unofficial capital." It is nestled in a long, narrow inlet that gives the impression of a safe haven, but which in reality offers scant protection at best. Exposed on the east to the ravages of the North Atlantic, Renews had borne the brunt of savage and sometimes devastating storms long before the arrival of the first European fishermen in the region.

On the night that William Jackman was born, the small settlement and its six hundred residents were being victimized by yet another of the many storms that occurred with regularity every year. Horizontal, driving rain, propelled by winds that at times approached eighty miles an hour, rattled like hailstones against windows and doors, drenching everything in its path. The few tiny lamps still burning were not visible for more than a few yards in the swirling blackness that enveloped the community. The roar of the wind muted the sound of the breakers crashing against the beaches and the rocks below. Neither man nor beast stirred outside.

Ironically, the day had dawned bright and clear with the promise of fair weather. By eight o'clock however it was evident to everyone in the community that a storm was in the making. Menacing black clouds had darkened the sky and a brisk wind blew long spumes of mist from the whitecaps that rolled relentlessly toward shore, increasing in size and momentum. By noon, the winds were reaching gale force. Fishermen hurried to double check that their boats were securely fastened on their collars. As they went about their work and prepared for the stormy hours ahead, the men and women of the community kept a wary eye on the degenerating weather. Those who had someone near and dear to them somewhere out on the water were painfully aware that gales like this had claimed more ships and the lives of more men than they cared to contemplate. By early afternoon, the storm was in full fury.

The people of Renews, like those of the hundreds of other outport communities that dot Newfoundland's twenty-five hundred miles of coastline, always had great respect for the elements. With the wisdom bred by constant exposure to the worst that the North Atlantic had to offer, they knew how to weather storms on land or sea, and how to survive. The instinct for survival in this harsh environment engendered in many Newfoundlanders an extraordinary ability to judge the weather. Every day they made life and death decisions based on the look of the sky, the feel of the wind, and their own intuitive sense of what the coming hours or days would bring.

This storm, like many of the severe storms that occur in Newfoundland each year, had its origin thousands of miles to the south. Hurricanes born in the hot, moist air of the South Atlantic have wreaked devastation on the world since time began. These monstrous storms can generate winds of almost two hundred miles per hour, blinding torrential rains, and ocean tides capable of creating coastal flooding of mammoth proportions. They are unpredictable. There is no set pattern to their behaviour. Sometimes a newborn hurricane will start out with great force toward land only to curl back and meekly fizzle out from whence it came. Others will persist in their charge toward land, gathering strength and momentum as they travel, seeking out their favourite targets in South America, the Gulf of Mexico, Florida, and the Carolinas.

Occasionally a hurricane will turn northward after venting its rage in the south. Usually, by the time it meets the colder air of the Labrador Current, it is diminished, and merely subjects the island to a few more days of the rain, drizzle, and fog that characterizes Newfoundland's coastal climate. The occasional hurricane however, although seemingly spent, will somehow find renewed life in the North Atlantic and the unfortunate communities that lie in its path are often punished mercilessly for days, sometimes with devastating and tragic consequences.

Equally deadly are the sudden squalls that develop locally when the right combination of meteorological conditions combine to spawn their existence. Newfoundland's history is replete with the loss of thousands of ships and boats of all sizes, and men who perished in great numbers when unexpected storms arose so suddenly and with such ferocity that the overwhelmed mariners were helpless to defend themselves. The poignant ballad, "The Petty Harbour Bait Skiff," records for posterity the drowning of six young men and boys returning from Conception Bay on a beautiful, calm day in June with a load of bait when their small boat, unable to withstand the wrath of a sudden summer squall, capsized and sunk.

With a stoicism that has always characterized them as a race, Newfoundlanders have learned how to mourn and accept the deaths of loved ones lost to the sea. More importantly perhaps, they have learned how to keep the memory of lost sons, brothers, and husbands alive with the endless telling and retelling of stories about their lives and times.

Silas Power, the shopkeeper, had watched the progress of the storm all day. Around five o'clock he said to his wife Sadie, "Mind the store, I'm going to try to get the horse into the stable. If I don't, God only knows where I'll have to go to get him in the morning."

Sadie involuntarily tugged her shawl a little tighter around her neck and shoulders as she watched Silas pull on his heavy clothes. She placed another junk of wood into the stove to curb the chill and draft that pervaded every nook and cranny of the old store. She checked the bucket she had earlier put under the leak that threatened to damage some of the store goods resting on the floor behind the counter. It was already over half-filled. It would need to be emptied several times before the storm passed. She would keep the shop open for another hour or so in case someone from the community needed something, but she knew that it was unlikely that anybody would venture out in this weather unless there was an emergency of some sort.

In the house furthest out on the point, George and Mary Sullivan were going about their usual evening routine. Mary, in her mid-seventies, stirred the fish and potatoes that would be their meagre supper while George, eighty-two, trimmed the lantern that he would later hang in the window upstairs. Brother and sister, neither had ever married. Both had lived their entire lives in this old house that creaked and groaned continuously. Every gust of wind caused it to tremble on its wooden shores.

Mary had been deathly afraid of storms as a child. Seeking the comfort of her mother's arms, she would cover her eyes and burrow deeply into her mother's bosom or under the quilts on the bed, pretending that the storm outside did not exist. Even now she sometimes still held her breath until the blast of wind that shook the glass in her bedroom window had passed. Even though the window, after all these years, had never yet broken, Mary could never quite bring herself to believe that it would not shatter with the very next gust. On stormy days and nights like this she kept herself occupied with her sewing and knitting, or sometimes she simply held the Bible that she couldn't read.

Laying down the pipe that he had held unlit between his teeth for the past hour or more, George mounted the stairs to hang the lantern. He had done this every night without fail for the last fifty years, carrying on a tradition started by the grandfather he could no longer remember. Even on the clearest of nights it was doubtful that the lantern would be visible for any great distance. Any vessel in distress would have to be perilously close to shore indeed to see it in time to avert tragedy. Nevertheless, George performed this little task of mercy each night, taking at least some small comfort in the fact that "even a tiny light like mine is better than ne'er one a'tall."

As they sat for their evening meal, Mary offered the same blessing that she had said for all of her adult life. George laid his still unlit pipe on the table next to his plate. Their only concession to the storm outside was the extra supply of wood and water that George had brought in earlier in the day. They both hoped it would last them until the storm passed.

Several houses away, Catherine Jackman and her older sister, Louise Power, sat and talked in the warmth of the kitchen. Louise, leaving her two sons and ten-year-old daughter in the care of their grandmother, had made the long trip up from Trepassey three days earlier to be with Catherine as she neared the end of her first pregnancy. Upon her arrival, Louise, "Aunt Looie" to all who knew her, announced that she had come "to show my poor little skiver[3] of a sister how to bring her first child into the world. I don't know how she'd ever manage to do it without me here to help her."

It was six o'clock. Catherine sat in the rocking chair holding a skein of new sheep's wool over her outstretched arms which Louise, facing her on a small stool, was twisting into a ball with a dexterity that showed she had done this many times before. They were alone in the big old house, both conspicuously aware of the storm that raged outside. During one particularly violent gust of wind Catherine murmured, "How I wish Thomas was here." She wasn't sure whether her words were spoken in reference to the storm outside or to the labour pains that had started earlier that morning.

Both Louise and Catherine were oddities in their respective communities. They were *townies*, born and raised in St. John's.

Each had married a man from the Southern Shore and had moved there to start a new life and raise their families. Unlike her small and slender sibling, Louise was a vigorous, heavy-set woman, fourteen years her sister's elder and was as much at home on a fish flake or in a dory as she was in her own kitchen. She had married early at the age of seventeen and had adapted so quickly and so readily to the outport way of life in Trepassey that the people of the community soon forgot that she was a townie. In fact, her transformation from *townie* to *bayman* was so complete that Louise herself now routinely displayed the open scorn and disdain that most outport people reserved for their cousins in St. John's. She even forsook the prim and proper speech that she had spoken in the capital city, and lapsed into the rich Irish brogue of the men and women born and raised on the Southern Shore.

In the second year of their marriage, her husband Jacob had managed to get a job as a fish culler and general handyman with Hutchings Brothers, a fishing firm based in Trepassey. His job kept him close to home, seldom requiring him to venture from shore. Thus, Louise rarely experienced the long, lonely hours or the worry and dread that the wives of fishermen and other seafarers felt as their men plied their trade on the treacherous seas. Still, she had a great affinity for these women and was among the first to be at their sides to comfort them in times of sorrow or distress. Her compassion and generosity were well-known to everyone in the community, and people were quick to call upon her when they needed help or consolation. She was never known to refuse.

Because of her relative newness to the community, Catherine was still a townie to the people of Renews. Nevertheless, they had immediately accepted her as "Tom's girl," and in the space of a few short weeks she had made a small circle of friends. Some of them tried to coach her in the ways of outport life. Her keen interest in wanting to learn and her genuine, but sometimes funny and futile, efforts quickly endeared her to these work-hardened women. Thus the shy young woman from St. John's soon became one of their favourite "sisters."

Catherine glanced at the clock, noting that it was nearing 8:00 p.m. "I think I'll make us another cup of tea," she told Louise, still thinking how nice it would have been for Tom to be at home for the birth of their first child. But as she rose from her chair to put the kettle on the stove, her body was seized with a sudden spasm of pain that brought instant sweat to her brow and the palms of her hands. She gripped the arms of the chair with whitened knuckles and it was several seconds before the pain passed. "I think it's time to go for Aunt Maggie," she quietly told her sister. Louise nodded in agreement.

Before leaving, Louise moved the two large kettles of water that had been warming on the back of the stove to the front dampers where they could quickly be brought to a boil. She placed the cloths and rags that she had collected and washed earlier in the week on the small washstand that stood by the side of Catherine's bed, making sure that all would be in readiness when Aunt Maggie arrived. Twenty minutes later she returned with the woman in tow, both of them soaked to the skin by their quick dash through the storm.

"Now Catherine, my dear, let's get you straightened out. We got a lot of work ahead of us. But don't worry, it'll be over before you know it, and you'll have a nice little bundle for Tom when he gets home."

Between them, Louise and the community midwife, known by all as Aunt Maggie, managed to get Catherine up the stairs and into her bed. The three women settled in for what they knew might be a long night. They talked, mostly Louise recounting in vivid detail her own pregnancies years earlier, puttering around the room as she did so. Louise's enormous store of nervous energy, which even in her most relaxed moments would not permit her to remain still for long, now compelled her to spring from her chair every few minutes to fuss with the items on the washstand or to tidy up whatever happened to lie in her eye's path. She chattered incessantly as she did so. At one point she went downstairs and spent several long minutes outside, watching the storm from the shelter of the front porch overhang, getting slightly wet and more than a little chilled in the process.

Aunt Maggie, unlike Louise, sat quietly and calmly in the old rocking chair that stood in the corner of Catherine's and Thomas' bedroom. She contributed occasionally to the conversation, but most of the time just listened, sometimes dozing off for a minute or two. She wanted to conserve her energy and be at her best when the time came.

Childless herself, Aunt Maggie had assisted in the birth of practically every child born in Renews during the past thirty years or so. Her life had not been an easy one. She had been both a bride and a widow in the same year, at the tender age of eighteen. Five months after her marriage to James O'Brien from Cappayhayden, another small community four miles south of Renews, her young husband had died of blood poisoning complications while on a fishing trip into Placentia Bay. A rusty spike had penetrated his rubber boot with such force that it had emerged through the top of his foot. Maggie could never understand how she knew in the early hours of the morning, long before his schooner brought him back to shore, that something was dreadfully wrong. Her worst fears were confirmed later that day when his schooner landed and the men lifted James onto the wharf. Maggie tried to talk to him, but in his fever and weakened condition, he didn't even recognize her. Despite the frantic efforts of everyone to save him, the ugly purple lines that radiated from the wound on his foot were so far advanced that they could not be arrested. Within a week, he was dead.

For several days, Maggie was so numbed with shock that she was unable to comprehend the fact that James was gone forever from her life. When the reality of his death finally sunk in, her grief consumed her night and day. The weeks and months that followed were spent in a semi-stupor of hopeless misery in which she was hardly aware of what was happening around her. Maggie stayed with the O'Briens for another eight months. She and James had moved in with them immediately after the marriage and had planned on making a start on their own home in the fall when the fishing season was over. The O'Briens shared her grief in the loss of their only son. They comforted her as best they could, but mostly they left her alone to mourn in her own way. When she told them that she was leaving, they pleaded with her to stay. But Maggie now realized that she was only an added burden to them in their own impoverished circumstances and served no purpose other than to perhaps fill some emotional void in their sad and lonely existence. She returned to Renews to live once again with her mother Bride.

The two women, daughter and mother, both widows, lived alone. Their house, next to the Roman Catholic cemetery, had been built by Maggie's father many years earlier. It had once been one of the better houses in the community but now stood in constant need of liming and repair. They somehow managed to eke out a thread-bare existence by bartering knitted and baked goods for food and other necessities. The community did its best to help out the two women whenever it could. The community needed them, for Bride was its mid-wife and "doctor." The fresh fish that a fishermen would occasionally drop off supplemented the few vegetables that Bride and Maggie managed to grow in the little garden between their house and the graveyard. When cutting out a meal of cod tongues or sounds for their own families, some women would often slice out a few extra for Bride and Maggie. The sacks of blueberries, partridgeberries, and bakeapples that they picked on the nearby barrens also constituted a large part of their year-round diet. Sometimes Maggie would earn a little extra by tending to the children of the widower, Captain Isaac Power, when he was away at sea. They survived.

Whenever Bride went out on her missions of mercy, Maggie would accompany her. Over a period of months and years, she too gradually learned the ancient art of mid-wifery by watching and helping her mother perform her duties. When Bride died sixteen years later, it was assumed without question by everyone in the community, and by Maggie herself, that the daughter would continue on in the mother's stead.

Like her mother, Maggie also developed a great passion for learning the cures and medicines of outport Newfoundland. She was a keen student of the age-old remedies passed on to her by her mother. Continually she strove to broaden her knowledge through reading and, whenever she had the opportunity, through discussions with other men and women from neighboring communities. With the passage of time, she acquired an extensive repertoire of cures and treatments, and the people of Renews looked to her for help with their injuries and illnesses.

Armed only with poultices, a supply of clean rags, her own herbal potions and ointments, and a dauntless spirit, she went forth whenever she was called upon. She sewed up their cuts, set broken bones, lanced their boils, sucked out deadly poisons, and did whatever else she could do to ease their pain and suffering.

Most of the ingredients that she needed for her herbal mixtures came from her own tiny herb garden. She grew feverfew, mint, "heal-all," and a few other herbs and plants that were known to have healing properties. Others, like camomile and tansy, she gathered from the surrounding countryside.

Interspersed with her practical remedies were some of the ancient rituals and superstitions that have characterized folk medicine everywhere. She could never quite bring herself to believe, however, that the passing of a golden ring seven times over a sty on someone's eye, or the rubbing of a piece of salt pork over warts in the light of a full moon would work. Yet she had seen the results of such pagan rituals too many times to discount them entirely.

The pain and suffering which accompanied broken bones, arthritis, severed limbs, and countless other injuries and illnesses, were accepted as a normal part of life. One of the most prevalent and sometimes hardest to endure, although not life threatening, was a toothache. It afflicted young and old alike. A hot plate or saucer held to the side of the face or a bit of frankum placed on the exposed nerve of a tooth sometimes offered temporary relief. The only real cure, however, was to have the bad tooth, or teeth, extracted. This was one area where Aunt Maggie could not help them; she simply did not have the physical strength to do it.

Maggie never forgot the circumstances of James's death nor her feelings of despair and helplessness. She had not been able to treat him, and, in the end, had not even been able to comfort him in his delirium. It would haunt her forever that she didn't even have the chance to tell him goodbye. Even though many years had since passed, every time she was confronted with some wound that threatened to fester, she vividly relived the experience of James's passing.

Still, on at least three occasions she had somehow managed to push aside her emotions to successfully treat wounds that were obviously and perilously close to blood-poisoning. One of them had been a foot wound almost identical to the one that had taken her husband away.

Now nearing her sixtieth year, she was sometimes saddened by the fact that she had no one to whom she could pass on this knowledge and responsibility. Years later, this fear would be alleviated when Catherine Jackman's oldest daughter, Johanna, showed herself to be an apt and willing student of the homeopathic medicines of Newfoundland under Aunt Maggie's tutelage and guiding hand.

Aunt Maggie was lost in her own thoughts when she suddenly realized that Catherine was growing more restless by the minute. Then she heard the young woman sigh, "Oh Aunt Maggie, why is it taking so long? I've been at it since early this morning, and it's now almost eleven o'clock. I'm so tired."

The labour pains that were now occurring with increasing frequency were not yet quite as bad as the first one she had experienced earlier that day. Catherine knew they would get worse, probably much worse, before it was over and vowed to herself that no matter how hard the pains became, she would not scream. As a small girl of ten, she had lain alone in her bed listening to her mother scream through the night. She had been certain that her mother was dying. She still remembered the intense fear and panic she had felt at the time. It wasn't until she heard the wail of her new-born brother in the early hours of the morning and her mother's gentle laugh that she had finally been able to drift off to sleep.

"Now Catherine, my darling girl, don't fret. Everything is going fine. Just try to rest. Don't worry, the baby will come when it's good and ready." The old woman's voice lent calmness and reassurance. She had been through this many times before.

Forty minutes later the pains began in earnest. Catherine gasped, her body freezing to rigid attention each time they struck. She had never felt anything even remotely close to this before in her life. Perspiration covered her entire body. Her long dark hair was plastered to the sides of her head, saturating the pillow and sheets beneath her. Each wave of pain was so excruciating that she sometimes drifted in and out of awareness. She was sure that she was dying and called out Thomas' name several times. Hearing a loud scream, she dimly realized that it was her own. She didn't care that she had broken her earlier resolve not to do so.

"Come on, girl. You can do it. You got to try harder. Harder now, come on, that's it. Come on." Aunt Maggie's voice now, for the first time, conveyed a sense of urgency and desperation. Louise, silent for one of the very few times in her life, continuously wiped away the perspiration that covered Catherine's face.

Eight minutes later, just twenty-three minutes before midnight, William Jackman was born, bellowing and flailing his tiny arms and legs to announce his arrival to the rest of the world. Aunt Maggie gently wrapped the baby boy after first thoroughly examining him to make sure that he had "all his little fingers and toes." Catherine gazed in awe and wonder at the tiny beet-red face of her first-born child for a long time, before tenderly cradling his tiny body in the crook of her arm. Within seconds, both the exhausted mother and her infant son were fast asleep, both oblivious to the storm that still raged around them.

Finally daylight broke, and the wind moderated to a brisk southerly breeze. Patches of blue broke the monotony of the steel-grey sky. The tides still ran extremely high, sending huge waves crashing against the cliffs and onto the beaches. But this was the normal aftermath of most severe wind-storms, and while it might be another day or two before fishermen could safely venture out in their small boats again, the storm was over. Renews and its people had escaped unscathed, and life quickly returned to normal. The only lasting impact on the community was a one-person increase in its population.

Having finished a second cup of tea, unusual for her, Aunt Maggie returned to her own home. Before leaving she gave Catherine and Louise a long litany of instructions on the proper care and feeding of newborn babies and their mothers. Within minutes, the news of William's birth began to circulate around the community, and before the day was out, most of Catherine's friends and in-law relatives dropped by to see her and her child. Some brought gifts of bread and jam, or a little something for the baby.

It would be another three weeks before Thomas Jackman met his first-born son. Catherine was waiting, with William in her arms, as her husband's schooner pulled into the wharf. When he pulled aside the blanket to see the tiny face scowling out at him, Thomas, never one for long speeches, merely chuckled and gave a short grunt of approval. Taking Catherine by the hand, he led his small family away from the wharf and up the hill to their home.

The town of Renews, birthplace of Captain William Jackman, circa 1900.

With the permission of the J.R. Smallwood Centre for Newfoundland Studies.

38 Eldon Drodge

The Jackmans of Renews

I'SE THE B'Y THAT BUILDS THE BOAT,
AND I'SE THE B'Y THAT SAILS HER!
I'SE THE B'Y THAT CATCHES THE FISH
AND TAKES 'EM HOME TO LIZER.

—"I'se the B'y"
Author unknown

Thomas Jackman, the proud new father, was a fifth-generation grandson of a William Jackman and his wife, Johanna, who had come ashore in Renews from a shipwreck in 1637, bringing with them nothing but the wet clothes that they wore. Having lost everything they owned in their aborted voyage to the New World, they had no means of going any further and thus had no alternative but to stay in the small community with the dozen or so families who already lived there. William had been a shopkeeper on the Isle of Wight, England, and was ill-prepared for the challenges that confronted him in his new circumstances. Left with no other choice, however, he adjusted quickly and erected a crude but effective shelter, learned to fish, chop wood, gather berries, hunt, and to do everything else that survival in this strange new environment demanded. Somehow making it through that first bitter winter, the Jackmans prevailed and prospered. Eventually they built for themselves the sturdy house in which the first Jackman children of Newfoundland would be born and raised.

Johanna was at William's side in everything that he did. She was an educated woman and, as time passed, was appalled by the

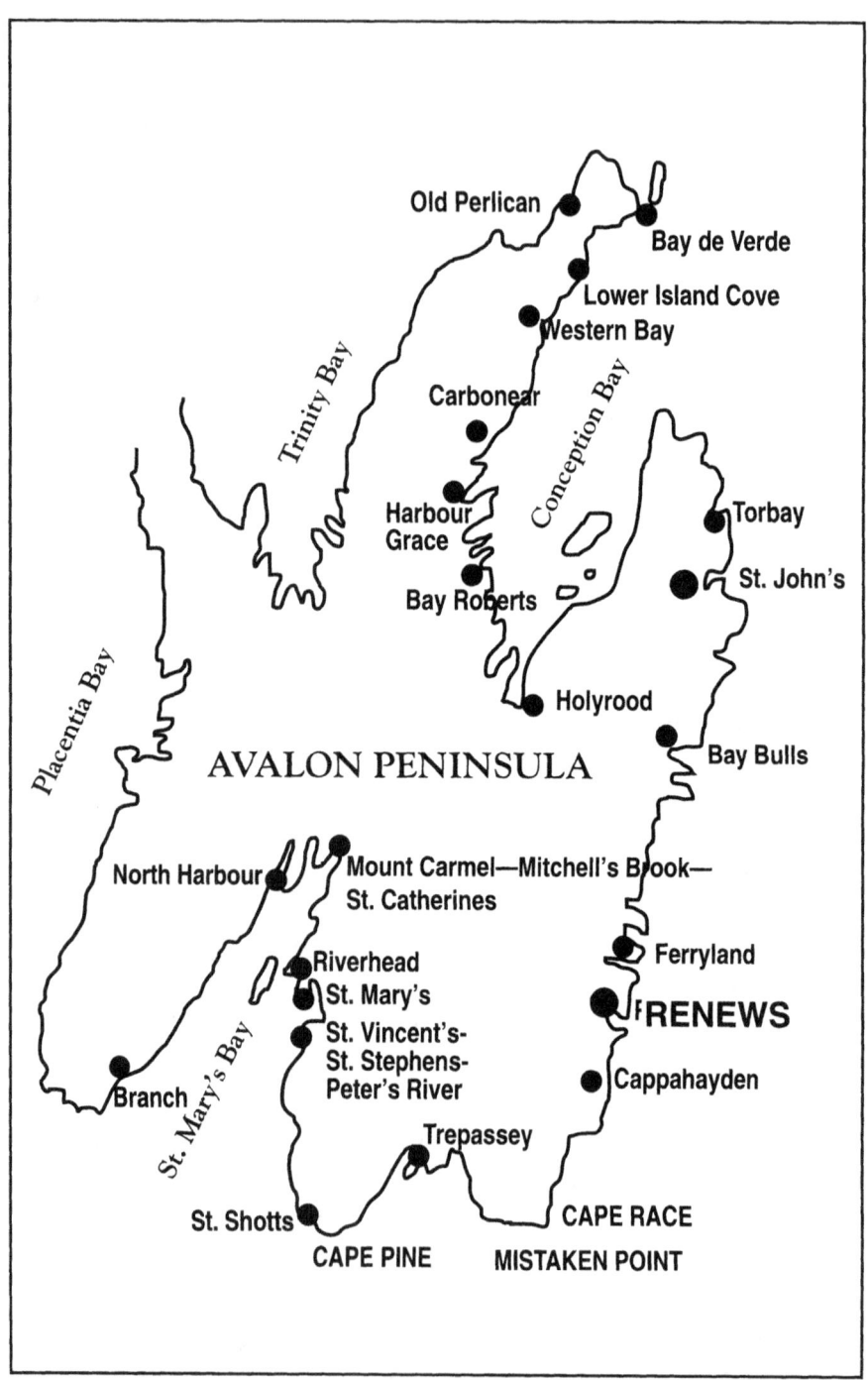

Old Perlican

Bay de Verde

Lower Island Cove

Western Bay

Trinity Bay

Carbonear

Conception Bay

Harbour Grace

Torbay

Bay Roberts

St. John's

Holyrood

Placentia Bay

Bay Bulls

AVALON PENINSULA

North Harbour

Mount Carmel—Mitchell's Brook— St. Catherines

Riverhead

Ferryland

St. Mary's

RENEWS

St. Vincent's- St. Stephens- Peter's River

Branch

Cappahayden

St. Mary's Bay

Trepassey

St. Shotts

CAPE RACE

CAPE PINE

MISTAKEN POINT

illiteracy and ignorance that she saw all around her. She had William construct an addition to their house which would serve as a small schoolroom for any children in the community whose parents would let them attend. In so doing, she became the first teacher recorded in Newfoundland history. Succeeding generations of Jackmans have maintained the strong traditions of their forebears and have contributed more than their fair share of the province's educators, captains, doctors, nurses, business people, and upstanding citizens in all walks of life.

A hundred and sixty years later, the blood of the original William and Johanna still flowed freely in the veins of the energetic, daring and ambitious Thomas Jackman. He had worked at various jobs around the community from the age of eleven. Then, at the age of fourteen, he joined the fishing industry. Even though he worked hard and did everything that was required of him, he, like all other first-year boys, received only a quarter-share for his season's work, and thus had very little to show for his efforts. After only one season, Thomas, at his young age, was intelligent enough to realize that a life of hardship and poverty lay ahead unless he did something different. He already knew what he wanted. The thought of someday owning and operating his own schooner possessed him, and he dedicated his time and energies over the next several years to making his dream a reality.

Four years later, just two weeks after his eighteenth birthday, he made the first real step toward his eventual goal when he launched the *Little Osprey*. She was a stout fifteen-ton, two-masted, schooner-rigged bully[4] about thirty-five feet in length. He had built her himself. It had taken him almost two years to cut the timbers that he needed, and to haul them from the woods to the grassy knoll just above the beach where he would eventually lay her keel. He had spent almost one entire winter combing the nearby woods for crooked black spruce suitable for her stem and ribs. When he wasn't fishing with his father, he spent every available hour working on her, sometimes at night by the light of an oil lantern hung on a nearby post. Although he was sorely tempted, only his fear of the reaction of his family and the rest of the community prevented him from working on Sundays. A couple of the older and more experienced boat builders of the community offered him advice from time to time, and he occasionally received a little help from some others. But in the end he could truthfully say that he had built her from stem to stern with his own hands. Even though he afterwards saw many things that he would do differently if he were starting over again, the *Little Osprey* was a remarkable achievement for such a young and inexperienced builder. Despite her rough construction and flaws, she would serve him well for the next five years and help him to eventually realize his dream of owning a full-size schooner.

Through the influence of an uncle living in St. John's, he managed to enter into an arrangement with Bowring Brothers, one of St. John's biggest fish merchants, to collect fish for them from inshore fishermen along the St. John's Shore. The owners of the firm were impressed enough with this brash young man to take a chance on him. He didn't disappoint them. The *Little Osprey* was ideally suited to this type of work and Thomas worked hard to make sure that he lived up to his end of the bargain in every respect. He recognized the value and benefits of work like this in contrast to life as an inshore fisherman and did everything within his power to prove his worth to Bowrings and others.

Sometimes, when the *Little Osprey* was not carrying fish, she was used to deliver freight. Thomas had convinced Bowrings that he could deliver their freight more economically to the communities near the St. John's Shore than they could themselves with their own larger and costlier schooners. Bigger and stronger than most men and willing to take on any task, his efforts did not go unnoticed, and he quickly became a well-known figure in the local fishing communities.

It was during his second year of operating the *Little Osprey*, at the age of twenty, that he first met the woman who would eventually become his wife. Having unloaded a cargo of fish in St. John's, he was delayed in making his departure while waiting for a supply of outward-bound freight to be delivered to the wharf. With time on his hands, Thomas left the vessel and took a leisurely walk along Water Street, something that he rarely did, usually preferring instead to stay with his vessel and the company of his two shipmates.

Strolling westward, he paused occasionally to look into shop windows or to chat with some acquaintance that he met along the way. His wandering eventually found him in front of a small shop at the extreme end of St. John's busiest street. The sign that said "Tools and Hardware; Proprietor H.M. Johnson" reminded him to get some brass screws that he needed for a few repairs on the *Little Osprey.*

It took a while for his eyes to adjust to the dimly lit interior of the store. He noted that store goods of every nature hung in disarray from the ceiling. Customers had to be careful when navigating the premises lest they strike their heads against the lower hanging objects. The wall shelves were crammed almost to overflowing, seemingly with little or no regard for the organization of the goods placed on them. The crowded counter left only a very small space in which Thomas could transact his business with the small, dark-haired girl standing behind it.

She smiled at him as she handed him his purchase. There was no one else in the store at the time, so Thomas spent a few pleasurable moments chatting with the young woman, discerning in that brief time that she was Catherine Johnson, the daughter of the store's owner.

By the time Thomas returned to his vessel, the freight that he was waiting for had finally arrived. It was quickly loaded and the little bully soon pulled away from the wharf. Within the next year and a half, the *Little Osprey* made many more trips to St. John's. Each time, Thomas made it a point to visit the tiny store at Water Street's west end. By the third or fourth visit, he was smitten with Catherine Johnson, and she with him. In the fall of 1835, at the age of twenty-two, he returned to Renews accompanied by Catherine as his wife.

A year later, Thomas finally realized his dream of owning his own full-size schooner. Through careful management of the proceeds from the operation of the *Little Osprey*, he was able to acquire the *Mable II*, an eighty-foot, seventy-five-ton schooner. He promptly renamed her the *Fanny Bloomer* after the phantom pirate ship that many claimed still roved the waters of the Southern Shore. He ignored everybody's warning that to rename a ship, especially after one so infamous, was to invite bad luck. The success he achieved over future years with his new vessel proved them all wrong. Within the short space of another two years, he established his own fishing business with premises in Renews and on Spotted Island in Labrador. He maintained his relationship with Bowring Brothers and, in addition to operating his own business, continued to buy fish and deliver freight for them for many years.

It was a good time in Thomas' life. His business was succeeding, and he knew that he always had a loving wife waiting for him whenever he came home. Catherine indeed loved Thomas dearly and cherished every moment that they spent together. In the first months of their marriage, however, she had quickly come to the realization that life as the wife of a mariner would not be an easy one. The days and weeks that Thomas spent at sea were the longest and the loneliest that she had ever known. Used to the hustle and bustle of her father's shop, there was now not enough activity to fill her days. As much as she yearned for the company of the few women in the community that she knew well, her natural shyness and fear of disrupting their work caused her to hesitate in calling on them. The few times that she had done so had been enjoyable experiences, and she had lingered each time over a second cup of tea, stretching out her visit as long as she dared. Even though she didn't realize it, these other women, worn and hardened by the challenges of their daily lives, enjoyed Catherine's company too. They particularly enjoyed listening to the interesting things that she told them about life in St. John's. Some of them often found time in their own busy workdays to drop into the Jackman home for a cup of tea. Mostly, however, they came to check on Catherine when Thomas was away at sea. They seemed to feel some sort of responsibility for this timid young woman from St. John's.

The long, lonely nights were what Catherine dreaded most of all. When she finally confided to one of the other women that she was afraid of sleeping alone in the creaky old house, the woman had immediately volunteered her oldest daughter to stay with Catherine each night. Catherine accepted the offer until she finally realized that she could not continue to rely on others in this manner for the rest of her life. Steeling herself every night to climb the stairs to her lonely bedroom, she slept fitfully at best. Every small sound brought her abruptly to full alert. The first faint rays of daylight filtering in through her bedroom window each morning always came as a blessed relief.

Catherine missed the life that she had known before moving to Renews. She missed her father's shop and the smells and the hubbub of the St. John's waterfront. She longed to again play the small organ that she hoped she would someday inherit. Ironically, she even missed the dreadful afternoon tea parties of her mother that she had detested so much as a young girl.

However, with a grittiness that belied her frail appearance, she made a brave and genuine effort to adapt to her new environment, determined to be the best wife that she could possibly be to her husband. It was not until infant William arrived a year and a half later, however, that her life would finally become complete.

The family that Thomas and Catherine would eventually raise was, like most other families of the time, relatively large. In their lifetime the Jackmans would rear seven children: five boys and two girls. An eighth child died in infancy, living only a few days.

William, the firstborn, was an only child for two and a half years. Then, over the space of six years, he was joined in the world by brothers Michael, James, and Arthur. Two years later, the four boys had their "noses broken" by the arrival of sister Johanna. Later would come Lawrence and Mary. They would all do the Jackman name proud.

Catherine had great expectations for her children. She was determined to do everything in her power to help them transcend the circumstances that condemned most young people in the area to a life of poverty and hardship.

Young boys, uneducated and often totally illiterate, routinely joined fishing crews at twelve or thirteen years of age, leaving their childhoods behind. Girls married early, usually by the time they were sixteen or seventeen, sometimes even younger, to spend the rest of their lives raising children and helping their husbands eke out a living as best they could. Many women would never in their lifetimes venture beyond the communities in which they were born and raised.

A few young men and women managed to escape the life of toil and hardship that otherwise awaited them by entering the priesthood or convents. The vast majority of the others were left with no alternative but to try to wrest a dreary living from the cold, hostile waters of the North Atlantic. Once started, most men would spend their remaining days on the water, while their wives supported them in every possible way on the shore.

It was a common practice in many large families, particularly on the predominantly Roman Catholic Southern Shore, to reserve at least one child for the church. The number of young men and girls entering the priesthood or convents from the shore probably surpassed that of any other area of the island. Mothers especially were always proud to claim that their son was a priest or their daughter was a nun. It gave them a special status in the community. William Jackman himself, however, had no inclination toward the priesthood and was always grateful that he was the firstborn in his family, as it was usually one of the younger sons that were chosen for this purpose. Still, many years later, one of William's own sons would be ordained and spend his adulthood as Father William Henry, faithfully serving the people of many parishes in Newfoundland.

Another occupation that offered some opportunity for aspiring young women was the "service." Girls who were lucky enough to get a job in the service were considered to be fortunate indeed by most other people. Serving as housemaids, servants, or chambermaids for the wealthy merchant families in St. John's and elsewhere in Newfoundland, strong girls from "around the bay" were greatly favoured for this type of work. Often a girl's employment with a family would be the beginning of a lifelong association. Even though the service was an honourable, respected and sought-after occupation, Catherine always encouraged her daughters, Johanna and Mary, to strive for something else. A big part of her motivation was knowing that if they left home to work in the service, she might only rarely, if ever, see them again, something that she could not bring herself to even contemplate.

None of her children fell short of Catherine's hopes and aspirations for them. Michael and James would spend most of their lives productively employed in the family fishing business. They both stayed a little closer to home than the others and were the "glue" that held together the business started years earlier by their father, Thomas.

Arthur, with his great sense of adventure, would become famous as "Viking Arthur" for his exploits as a prolific sealing captain and whaler and, perhaps more identifiably, as an explorer who accompanied Admiral Robert Peary on his first expedition to

Captain Arthur Jackman, famous brother of William Jackman.

the Arctic Circle in 1886. Like William, he grew to become a man of towering intellect and great courage. His strength, both physical and mental, was evident in an incident that occurred on one of his many sealing voyages as captain of the *Eagle*. When one of his fingers got accidentally caught in the ship's winch and was damaged beyond repair, he asked his chief engineer to cut it off for him. The man refused. Miles away from any form of medical help, Arthur took the axe without hesitation, chopped off the finger himself, bandaged it carefully, and went back to work.

Lawrence, the youngest son, unfortunately, never lived to reach his full potential. He died at the age of twenty. Mary, the youngest of them all, spent much of her adult life as a respected school teacher in St. John's.

Their sister Johanna was cast from the same mold as her original namesake—strong, determined, energetic, and instilled with enormous compassion for others. She would eventually become known as "Doctor Johanna" for her ministrations to the sick and injured of Renews and other nearby settlements. Following in the footsteps of Aunt Maggie, she developed great knowledge and skill in the homeopathic medicines and remedies of her time. She is perhaps best known for having once saved the life of a man severely injured and near death from shotgun wounds. The accidental blast had left severe powder burns and more than two dozenwounds over the man's upper body and face. Everyone except Johanna gave him up for dead. With persistence and ingenuity she treated him day and night, refusing to believe that she couldn't save him. Four months later, although scarred and maimed for life, the man was back on his feet, and Johanna's reputation as a healer was assured.

Thanks largely to Thomas Jackman's drive, initiative and inherent entrepreneurial abilities, the Jackman children never really experienced the full extent of the abject poverty and near-starvation that many other families of the area knew. Still, neither Thomas nor Catherine were blind nor indifferent to the poverty and hardship that existed all around them, and many of the poorest families in the community experienced at some time or other the Jackmans' generosity and kindness.

The Jackman children lived the normal life of most other boys and girls at that time. They played the same games, went to mass, and did the same chores. Like other children of the community, they too sometimes came home wet and freezing from their tumbles into the icy water when copying[5] or playing around the salt water. Rowing the punt around the harbour provided the opportunity for William and his brothers or some of the other boys to try to out-muscle each other and turn the boat from its normal course. Birthdays, Christmas, and visits to other nearby communities were always looked forward to. One of the highlights of the year for the Jackman children and the other children of Renews was the annual community picnic, usually held on the first or second Sunday in July. On this day, practically the whole community bundled into punts and skiffs, and made their way to one of the long stretches of beach just outside Renews Head where they all enjoyed a great outing by the sea.

Children, almost from the moment that they first learned to walk, were expected to do their share of the never ending toil and labour that survival in most of the island's towns and villages demanded. They grew up knowing that they had to work. They had no choice. Young William Jackman and his brothers were no exception. They quickly got into the routine of bringing water from the well, cleaving splits, carrying wood, shovelling snow, turning fish, weeding the potato garden, and doing the dozens of other tasks that were expected of them every day. After a while, they did these chores automatically without being asked or reminded. It was their job, their role in the functioning of the household, and they rarely attempted to shirk this responsibility.

Similarly, Johanna and Mary, like all other young girls, learned at a very early age how to do housework, wash and dry clothes, sew, knit, bake and cook, and help out their mother in every way that they could. In some families, especially where there were mostly females, young girls also did many of the chores normally done by boys. Once, when William teased Johanna by suggesting that she do some of the chores assigned to him, Catherine interceded and told him that that would be alright as long as he himself agreed to come in and cook their supper, scrub the kitchen floor, and mend the pile of clothes in the sewing basket. William declined and made no further overtures in that direction.

The calluses and lines of hard work were worn by many as a badge of honour. Auntie, who each year moved into the Jackman home for the winter months, claimed that she had worked every single day of her life. She always liked to boast, even into her late eighties, about her first trip to Labrador at the age of ten as a serving maid on a fishing schooner. With a touch of pride in her voice, she frequently told willing listeners that she was so tiny when she first worked on her father's schooner that she had to stand on a chair to knead the dough for the men's bread.

Work made children strong, both physically and emotionally. By the time most boys reached the age of twelve or thirteen, they had almost the strength of full grown men, their upper bodies, arms and shoulders so developed by the thousands of buckets of water that they had carried and the hard work that they did every day. Boys grew into men ready to take sole responsibility for themselves and the families that they would eventually have. They were prepared to do whatever it took to feed, clothe, and protect their wives and children for the rest of their lives.

Any person who was not prepared to work as hard as everyone else or as diligently as the community expected them to was quickly labelled as lazy or shiftless. Once applied, the tag rarely ever left them. In most cases, the nickname left no doubt about the person's shortcomings. In Renews, around the time of William's childhood, there were three men with the same name—Jim Power. One of them was known in the community as Jim of Patrick, another as Jim the Carpenter. The other was known as Lazy Jim. Never called anything else, the latter always responded when addressed in this manner as if it were the proper name given him at birth.

The true value of a child, however, did not lie in the extra pair of hands that its existence represented. In most families, children were cherished for themselves. They were their parents' most important and prized possessions. This was always clearly evident in the Jackman family where William and his brothers and sisters were loved and nurtured from birth, disciplined when they strayed, quickly forgiven, and placed above all else in importance.

However, it wasn't all work. The days of summer were rounded out with games and activities such as goolos[6], skipping, connoring, trouting, swimming, and many other games that the children made up themselves and played, usually until dark. Most children at that time had very few toys. The few that they did possess they made themselves or were made for them by a loving mother or father who could give them nothing better. William, like most boys, loved to shape small boats out of junks of wood, equip them with some sort of sail, and watch them float along the beach or across the harbour. Meanwhile, the Jackman girls and their friends played with homemade dolls dressed up in leftover pieces of cloth or whatever other materials they could lay their hands on. Sliding and snow fights were among their favourite winter pastimes. It was copying, however, with its attendant risk of a good wetting, that gave the children the most fun and excitement of all. William experienced his own share of falls into the icy winter water and the feel of his soaked clothes freezing on his young back. Whatever the season, most children were usually tuckered out when bedtime came and fell asleep as soon as their heads touched the pillow.

In between their chores and games, some children also spent an hour or two in school each day until they were ten or eleven years old, at which time schooling for most of them was over. Many, unfortunately, never saw the inside of a schoolroom in their lifetimes. Their parents didn't see what an education could possibly do for a man or boy out on the water in a skiff or for a woman raising children. Almost without exception, however, parents considered the well-being of their children's souls to be above all else, and made sure that their sons and daughters attended mass regularly and received religious instruction. Failure to do so was sure to bring a quick visit from the parish priest. Continued absence would cause them to become outcasts, shunned by the community in which they lived.

Unlike many other parents in Renews at the time, however, Catherine insisted that every child of hers attend school and receive an education. Sometimes her children cared less about their education than she did herself, especially the boys, perhaps with the exception of Michael who seemed to have a natural thirst and aptitude for learning. On many mornings, some of them, even the conscientious Johanna, were reluctant to go to the drafty old schoolhouse that alternated between freezing in the winter and stifling heat in the spring and summer. Only their fear of Catherine's wrath if they didn't go or, even worse, the fact that she might tell their father when he got home, kept them going on a regular basis. Sometimes they couldn't understand why they had to go when most of the other children didn't. They were also afraid of the crusty old nun who taught them, and who disciplined them severely for the slightest infraction. They were expected to sit straight on their benches and never as much as turn their heads while the lessons were being taught. William, because he fidgeted more in class than the others, frequently felt the pain of her pointer stick across his knuckles. The Jackman children had a tacit understanding between them that they would never let their mother know when any of them received such punishment, for they knew that her sympathies would lie entirely with the Sister. Despite all this, however, each of the Jackman children eventually completed the education that Catherine had intended for them. The schooling that William, along with his brothers and sisters, received in the small one-room schoolhouse, would serve him well in his later life as a sea captain, the first president of the Star of the Sea Society, and as a leader of the men who served under him.

A great love of music also ran deep in the Jackman family. While William himself was only a passable singer at best, his sister Johanna had a rich clear voice and was often asked to sing in church. His younger brother Michael had a natural talent for the button accordion and spoons. Friends and relatives often dropped by the Jackman home in the evening in the hope that he would play a tune or two for them. He was always more than willing to oblige them.

The Jackman family's love of music was not unique. The people of the shore all loved to sing and play. Music was their common bond and probably their greatest love. Anyone who couldn't carry a tune or master a musical instrument themselves simply listened and enjoyed the singing and music of others, keeping time with their hands and feet. A visitor from St. John's, attending one of these gatherings for the first time, was once moved by curiosity to ask, "Why are all those people lined up along the wall? Are they waiting to use the toilet or something?"

His host laughingly replied, "No, b'y, they're just waiting for their turn to sing for the crowd." Over the years, the Southern Shore in particular, has contributed far more than its proportionate share of Newfoundland's and Canada's most talented singers and musicians.

In 1847, the children of the Jackman family miraculously all survived the epidemic of diphtheria that swept through Renews. Many others were not as fortunate, and more than two dozen children and adults of the community died before the epidemic ran its course. It was a time when diphtheria, tuberculosis, meningitis, and other diseases claimed the lives of countless Newfoundland men, women and children. Drownings, childbirth, untreated wounds, and accidents took many others. While they were more fortunate than most, Thomas and Catherine Jackman, in the latter years of their life together, would experience the terrible agony and sorrow of losing a child when their youngest son, Lawrence, contracted tuberculosis and died before reaching his twenty-first birthday.

It wasn't until the cottage hospital system was implemented in the early 1900's, starting with the Seamen's Institute in Grand Bank, that the government of the day accepted any meaningful responsibility for the health and well-being of its outport citizens. Consequently, every outport community in Newfoundland had its share of orphaned children. Almost without exception, however, parentless children were immediately taken in by their aunts and uncles, or grandparents, or in many cases, by families not even directly related to them by bloodline. Invariably, orphans integrated so quickly and so readily into their adoptive families that they never considered themselves to be anything but full-fledged biological sons and daughters, sharing equally in all aspects of family life. Rare indeed was the child in outport Newfoundland that did not know a mother's loving care or a father's stern but loving guidance. On no less than three occasions did the Jackman family temporarily take into their home parentless children until permanent homes were found for them. While there, they were accepted and well-treated by William and the other Jackman children, none of whom saw anything strange or odd about this arrangement.

The concept of "family" has always been central to the way of life in Newfoundland's outport communities. In the absence of any effective method of birth control (which would not have been an option for Roman Catholic women in any case) and perhaps even more so in the belief that "many hands make light work," large families were the norm. As well, no household in outport Newfoundland was complete without an older person or two, usually an aging grandmother or grandfather, or some favourite aunt or uncle. Often too advanced in age or too infirm to live alone or fend for themselves, most elderly people nevertheless played an important role in the family environment. The Jackman home was no different. Auntie, whose real name was Mary Ellen Jackman, the widow of Thomas' long-departed brother, James, lived in the Jackman home intermittently for several years until her death at the age of eighty-one. During the spring and summer months, she lived with one of her own daughters in nearby Cappahayden. But each year when fall arrived, she returned to the Jackman house which she considered to be much warmer, and the presence of so many children and their antics helped her pass the cold winter months. While there, much of the upbringing and training of the Jackman children was often entrusted to her. Many adult men and women, if asked who had been the biggest influence in their lives would undoubtedly point to some older person, like Auntie, who had guided much of their early development.

Most old people, like children, were revered and respected, cared for, and then mourned for when they died.

However, the family did not begin and end with the immediate household. In reality, it extended through the community as a whole. Most children felt comfortable and secure in their community environment and instinctively knew that they would be welcomed in almost any house in the community. They referred to most adults, whether they were related to them or not, as "aunt" or "uncle." People shared the work that had to be done and supported each other in every way that they could. There were usually very few secrets in these small communities, and when there was a need, other families were more than willing to help. This help took many forms. When a household was beset by illness or some tragedy and unable to look after itself, someone made sure that they had enough chopped wood to keep the fire going and food and water until they were well enough to look after themselves again. When boats were lost to the elements or houses lost by fire, they helped each other rebuild. Seldom did anyone in distress have to ask for help. It was usually offered willingly by men and women who expected nothing more in return than to be treated in the same manner when their own time of need came.

Any family trying to go it alone would surely have perished. Only in numbers and by working together could the people of outport Newfoundland overcome the awesome obstacles that confronted them every day. Despite the constant state of poverty and hardship of most people, however, they freely shared what little possessions they had.

A well-known story about two Renews families tells the depth to which sharing, self-sacrifice, and compassion for others sometimes went. In a community where many constantly lived on the edge of starvation, the families of Albert Sullivan and Tobias Codner were among the "poorest of the poor." Nearing the end of a particularly harsh winter, the food reserves of Albert and Ethel Sullivan and their six children—all girls—were virtually depleted. They were down to their last quarter-sack of flour. Next door, the

Codners were literally starving to death. The only food left to sustain this family of seven consisted of a handful of dried tom-cods and a few frostbitten potatoes. To make matters worse, Codner had severely injured his leg while cutting wood and could not even rise from his bed. In despair his wife Julia confided to Albert that she had no idea where their next mouthful of food would come from and that she expected them to all be dead long before summer arrived.

Without hesitation, Albert shared the last of his small supply of flour with the Codner family. It was an act of extreme generosity by a compassionate and caring individual, but one that brought his own family perilously closer to the brink of starvation. A simple man, he trusted in God's will to see them through.

That very afternoon, Albert walked to the barrens, as he did on most days, to check the rabbit slips that he had set there the previous fall. Rabbits that are sometimes plentiful in autumn are for some reason almost impossible to snare during the winter and spring. Nevertheless, Albert checked his snares regularly and had been rewarded with fine hares a couple of times during the winter for his efforts. As he approached the last of his snares, he saw that one of them now contained a trapped animal. He could tell immediately that the animal lying dead in the snare was not a rabbit. To his utter amazement, he realized that it was a silver fox, a rare animal much valued for its precious fur.

The next day he made the twelve-mile trek to Ferryland where he was paid enough for the pelt to safely see his own family and the Codner's through the rest of the winter.

Long, work-filled days left little time for social interaction between the people of most outport communities. The main diversions from the hardship of their everyday lives were mass, weddings, wakes, and occasional gatherings called "times" that occurred throughout year. Times were usually held at Christmas or on some other special occasion or sometimes to simply celebrate the conclusion of a particularly bountiful fishing season. On the Southern Shore, the time held to celebrate St. Patrick's Day was undoubtedly the most popular of all. It was the one day of the year when the Irish roots of the people were most evident, and the gaiety, the games, the drinking, the dancing and singing, and everything else they did on that day made them all feel for a few hours that they were back on the Old Sod. Concerts, skits, and the inevitable card games usually rounded out the day.

The festivities were for everybody, young and old alike. The Jackman children always looked forward to these occasions with great anticipation of the games they would play and the food they would eat. It also gave William and his brothers the opportunity to have a dance with the girls of the community. Times were held in parish halls or any other buildings big enough to accommodate the large numbers of people that usually wanted to attend. In warm weather they were sometimes held outdoors as garden parties or "soirees."

It was one of the few times in the year when people treated themselves and forgot their cares and woes for a few hours. The array of sweets and desserts offered up for these gatherings was a delightful departure from their normal diet of fish, potatoes, bread, and strong tea. Women often hoarded the last of their precious supplies of berries, molasses, and sugar to contribute pies and other delicacies to the occasion. Some of the best "feeds" that William would always remember were the pies, cakes and plates of cookies that he and some of his friends managed to sneak outside to eat all by themselves. They gorged themselves during these rare opportunities to eat as much as they could.

Children were given free rein, and were permitted to stay up as long as they wanted. Most, however, fell asleep long before the party was over and had to be carried home in the arms of their parents in the wee hours of the morning. A common sight at any time was the mass of small bodies, blissfully oblivious to the noise and bustle around them, sleeping akimbo on a pile of coats in the far corner of the room. As an adult, William would still remember being led home in the eerie half-light of early morning, staying as close as possible to his mother and father as his eyes searched for the spirits and tokens that he knew lurked in every shadow.

It was also a rare opportunity for the men to relax from their work. Unfortunately, as in the well-known Newfoundland folk song, *The Kelligrew's Soiree*, the party would occasionally be marred when they drank a little too much and argued or fought with each other. "Rackets" like this were expected, perhaps even looked forward to by some people. One man who once made the long trip home to Trepassey from St. John's to attend his community's annual garden party went back disappointed. When he returned to his workplace in St. John's a few days later, he confided to his fellow employees "Sure it wudn't much of a party dis toime. Dere wuz no fights or nuttin." Even though many people enjoyed an occasional scuffle, the Jackman children had strict orders from Catherine to stay out of the way if the party got rough, and to never, under any circumstances, participate in any manner in such activities.

However, times, garden parties, and "soirees" were usually very happy affairs and for most people welcome, if brief, respite from the constant toil and labour of daily living.

Mummering was another favourite Southern Shore pastime. The earliest English settlers in Newfoundland brought with them the centuries old Christmas custom of disguising themselves and then visiting most of the homes in their communities in the hope of getting something to eat or drink. Adults anticipated and sometimes received, a drop of dark rum or a cup of homemade wine. Often, however, to their disappointment they were passed a mug of lemon crystals or syrup, sometimes accompanied by a piece of cake. Also called "janneying" in some areas, mummering spread to all parts of Newfoundland and Labrador and is still practiced today in many of the province's outport towns and villages, although on a much smaller scale.

Mummers went to great lengths to keep their identities secret. Men sometimes dressed as women, and women as men. Often they wore their long underwear on the outside to cover the clothing that would surely give away their identities. The rags that they sometimes used to cover their bodies camouflaged pillows or rolled-up quilts meant to change the contours of their frames. Most tried to speak in a high falsetto that they hoped nobody would recognize and wore masks or painted their faces to make themselves look as ugly and as fearsome as possible. All of the Jackman children always got great enjoyment out of trying to guess the mummers' identities, but it was Johanna, with her great sense of observation, who was most often correct. As they got older, they too went around the community mummering, and went to great lengths in planning their disguises.

Sometimes the mummers sang for their handouts or performed little skits in the hot kitchens whose floors threatened to collapse with their numbers. Small children sometimes watched these frightening creatures in fear and trepidation. Mothers and fathers everywhere, at any time during the year, could usually subdue their misbehaving children into obedience with the threat that "you better be good or the "Janney" will get you."

Unfortunately, the darker side of mummering gave some people the opportunity, under the immunity of their disguises, to take revenge for some earlier incident or mistreatment. Sometimes they would beat the individuals who had offended them or would damage their property. Mummering was eventually outlawed in Newfoundland in 1861 when a number of men, dressed as mummers, brutally murdered another man in Bay Roberts. While strictly enforced in St. John's and the area where the killing had taken place, the law was generally ignored everywhere else, and the practice continued as usual.

Despite occasional instances such as these, however, mummering and janneying helped to make the twelve days of Christmas one of the most enjoyable times of the year for the Jackman family, and for men, women and children all along the Southern Shore, many of whom had little else to brighten their yuletide season.

Growing Up

WHEN JACK GREW UP TO BE A MAN,
HE WENT TO LABRADOR.
HE FISHED IN INDIAN HARBOUR,
WHERE HIS FATHER FISHED BEFORE.

— "Jack Was Every Inch a Sailor"
Author unknown

Aunt Maggie, who had been present at the birth of each of the Jackman children, felt that she owned a small part of every child that she had helped bring into the world in her many years as the mid-wife of Renews. She remembered their names and their ages, and most of their birthdays. They were all welcomed guests in her house, and no child ever left her kitchen without a piece of jam-covered bread or some other small treat. Whenever diphtheria, scarlet fever or some other sickness carried away one of "her children," it also took with it a tiny piece of Aunt Maggie herself. She loved them all dearly and grieved deeply when they died.

As much as she loved the others, however, she reserved a special spot in her heart for William Jackman. She wasn't exactly sure why. Perhaps her affection for him had grown out of her close friendship with his mother. She loved him like the son she herself never had. And as he grew, William came to love this kind, old woman just as much in return. She was like a grandmother to him. She would say many times in her lifetime that she "knew William was special from the moment I first laid eyes on him. I don't know what it was. He was a big baby, almost nine pounds. But it wasn't that. There was something different about him. I could just feel it."

As a youngster, William was known throughout the community as "Captain Tom's boy." Like all other children in the extended family of the community, he knew that it was safe and acceptable for him to drop into most of the houses in Renews at any time. Most adults usually kept an eye on all the children playing around them, whether they were their own or not. No matter where he was, whenever the need overtook him, he would simply stop whatever he was doing and make for the nearest house to ask for a glass of water or, sometimes, a slice of bread. He was never refused. In his adult years, he would fondly remember the many pleasant hours he had spent in the kitchens of Renews, especially Aunt Maggie's. There, sipping on weak tea sweetened with a drop or two of molasses and listening to her endless stories, he absorbed without realizing it much of the wit and wisdom that the wise old woman imparted.

From the time that he was able to make his first tentative steps, he was drawn to the salt water. The wharves with their boats, and the beaches and landwashes were magnets that demanded his attention for most of his waking hours. At the age of two, he would spend countless hours floating little homemade boats along the beach or tossing small beach-rocks into the water. His favourite pastime was to run out after some receding wave only to scramble back a few seconds later, squealing, when the next incoming wave threatened to overflow his boots. Whenever it was time to leave, he always pestered his mother to let him stay a little longer.

When he was four years old, he was permitted to play alone or with some of the other children in the landwash where his mother could keep an eye on him from the vantage point of her kitchen window. At six he was more or less free to come and go as he pleased. The only stipulation was that his mother always insisted on knowing where he was going, who he was with, and what he had done.

His daily sojourns would find him in almost every nook and cranny of the community. As he grew older, however, an increasingly larger portion of his time would be spent on one of the wharves where, along with other boys and girls, he would participate in the age-old boyhood activity known as "connoring." The water around the fishing stages of Renews, like all Newfoundland fishing settlements, teemed with a variety of scavenger fish attracted by the discarded fish offal that littered the bottom around the stage-heads. Connors, a species of perch, were by far the most plentiful and the easiest to catch. Despite the sharp thorns on their backs and their fearsome appearance, they did not flail around when caught. Instead they curled into a tight half circle remaining relatively still, which made the removal of the fish-hook safe and easy. Before being caught, a connor might glide slowly past the baited hook several times, feigning disinterest, and then at the last second suddenly turn and dart to swallow the proffered bait. This curious action undoubtedly gave rise to the well-known Newfoundland expression "sly as a connor."

Sculpins were a different matter altogether and were to be avoided if at all possible. Despite their tiny bodies, the sharp thorns on their huge heads and backs, and their vigorous flailing when caught made them very difficult to separate from the hooks on which they were snagged. In truth, most small boys were a little bit afraid of them.

Besides connors and sculpins, "flatfish" (of the sole family) also frequented the waters around most wharves. Unlike other fish, however, they preferred to rest on the very bottom, camouflaging themselves in the offal and silt and were usually hard to detect, given away only by the occasional twitching of their tails as they tried to burrow deeper into the sludge. They were rarely caught because they simply showed little or no interest in the bait that was offered to them. The only sure way to catch a flatfish was to stab it with a boat-hook, fish-prong or jigger.

Occasionally a boy might also catch one of the large, ugly salt-water eels that sometimes swam by. With the natural cruelty of most young boys, live eels were often nailed to a fence post or the wall of some outbuilding in the superstitious belief that an eel, no matter what horrors were inflicted upon it, would not die until the sun went down. They also sometimes served a practical purpose. Quite often the long strips cut from a cured eel skin substituted for bootlaces and were even preferred by some who believed that they were stronger and would last longer.

None of the fish caught in connoring were ever eaten. They were usually thrown back into the water or left to rot on the rocks and beaches. Sometimes a few might be used by some fisherman to fertilize his potato garden or cabbage patch.

It was while he was connoring that William experienced his first "dunking." Leaning out over the wharf to free the fish-hook that had become snagged in one of the wharf's pilings, he lost his balance and, before he could catch himself, plunged headlong into the cold, briny water. A fisherman who happened to be working nearby heard the loud splash and William's shrill cries of panic and plucked the frightened boy from the water within a matter of a few seconds. Taken home, soaking wet, goose fleshed and shivering, he was mildly scolded by his mother as she towelled him off and dressed him in dry clothes. That night, as she tucked him into bed and made sure that he said his prayers, she again teased him gently about his misadventure. They both shared a chuckle about it before William snuggled down between the patchwork quilts and the feather mattress and fell asleep, the incident already pushed into the background of his young mind.

William's second dunking, which came only five weeks later, was a much more serious matter and came within a hair's breadth of claiming his life. It happened on a Sunday, the one day of the week when many of the fishermen of the community liked to rest from their normal tasks by gathering at the wharves to talk, smoke or chew tobacco, and generally relax. It was a nice warm day in late June, following a stretch of the cold, foggy weather that almost always seems to mark the arrival of the small fish known as caplin to the bays and coves of Newfoundland. Easily harvested in great quantities when they "rolled" up on the beaches, these tiny fish served many purposes. Sun-cured and salted, they formed an important part of the winter diet of many families. They were feed for their dogs, fertilizer for their vegetable gardens, and bait for fishermen when squid and other kinds of bait were not available. On this day, the stench of thousands of caplin rotting on the beaches outdid the usual smells of tar, fish offal, and brine.

Luckily for William, as it later turned out, one of the men ventured out to the edge of the wharf to empty his pipe into the water. When the man leaned out over the wharf, he was aston-ished to see the face of a small boy peering up at him from a depth of eight or nine feet below and whose arms were gesticulating wildly as he sent a steady stream of bubbles that rose to break the smooth surface of the water above. Frozen for an instant by the bizarre sight, the man swore loudly before he sprang into action.

Grabbing a gaff-hook that stood nearby, he used it to deftly snag the boy's clothing and pull him up to the surface. No one ever knew how long William had been down there or how he had gotten there in the first place. When they laid him face down on the wharf, his face and body were blue, and he showed no visible signs of life. The men worked feverishly over him for several long minutes, fearing as they did so that the young boy was too far gone to be revived. They employed the last resort remedy of rolling him, stomach down, over one of the barrels that lined the wharf. Finally, to their immense relief and surprise, the boy gave a little cough, and a second or two later a great mixture of water and vomit spewed from his mouth.

When they took him home, still weak and unable to walk unaided, his mother's first reaction, frightened when told the details of his mishap, was to scold him. She berated him merciless-ly for a full five minutes before the reality that she had almost lost her son sank in. Then she thanked the Lord and the Blessed Virgin for saving him, clasped him tightly to her breast and wept. She cried off and on for a full two hours, at times sobbing incon-solably.

His mishaps, however, did little to diminish William's passion for the salt water. The very next day he was out and about on his usual rounds as if nothing had happened. Reassuring his mother that he would be more careful from now on, he went on his way. From that day, every time William went out through the door Catherine always said a silent little prayer to the Blessed Virgin Mary for his safety.

Incidents like these, especially coming so close together, would have turned many young boys from the salt water forever. Its only effect on William, however, was to instill in him a deep and profound respect for the sea that would stay with him for the rest of his life.

As William grew in size, so did he in boldness and audacity. He was every bit as adventurous and daring as most other boys of his age. Yet he never exhibited the kind of recklessness and wild abandon that some of the others showed. The large dose of common sense that he was born with would see him through many perils in his lifetime. His daily wanderings among the cliffs, woods, and barrens of Renews would often bring him to the brink of some danger, but he somehow always seemed to know just how far he could go and, more importantly, when to stop. William knew little or no fear of most things. One exception was the priest whom he firmly believed could "turn him into a rat" or "send him to burn forever in the eternal flames of Hell." This was a common fear felt by many boys and girls at that time. It was instilled into them by parents who perhaps felt that their children should have the same fear and deep respect for the church that they themselves possessed, and who often used the threat of telling the priest when their children misbehaved.

By the time he was eleven, it was obvious to most people that William would probably be a big, strapping man when he reached his prime. That year too the people of Renews were given a glimpse into the character of the person who would in time, at the age of thirty, become famous throughout Newfoundland and Labrador as Jackman, the Hero.

The incident happened on a clear day in September when most of the men of the community were still out on the water fishing. When a young girl ran home screaming to her mother that "Blizzard is loose!", word quickly spread, and everyone rushed to gather in the children playing outside and to try to get their few sheep, lambs, and hens into the safety of their pens.

Blizzard was one of two work-dogs owned by George Doyle. They were used by Doyle in the winter to haul firewood from the nearby woods and barrens. When not working, the dogs were kept on chains underneath Doyle's store, where the floor of the building above them provided the only shelter that they ever knew. A mixture of Newfoundland dog and Labrador husky, these big, powerful animals were preferred by many men to the small shaggy ponies generally used for this type of work.

The other dog, Sailor, was the bigger, but gentler of the two. He would permit small children venturing near him to pat his head, and he would always respond to their pleas to "give me the paw" by raising his great forepaw to meet their tentatively outstretched hands. In contrast, Blizzard was lean and restless and had a mean, vicious disposition. Most of his time was spent endlessly pacing the length of his tether, snarling and baring his teeth to everyone who passed nearby. Only Doyle could handle him, and even he was careful never to make any sudden movements or loud noises whenever he was within striking distance of those great jaws.

Once before Blizzard had broken loose from his chain. Before being recaptured, he had killed a sheep and sent a sharp jolt of fear through the entire community. He was still alive only because Doyle, who knew the true value of the dog in the winter woods, had compensated the sheep's owner for the loss. He also did it out of a sense of loyalty to the animal that had once saved his life. Doyle would never forget the winter day, three years earlier, when he had been overtaken by a sudden blizzard while cutting firewood miles from the community. In the swirling white-out conditions of the storm, unable to see more than a few feet in front of him, he had calmly perched himself on top of the few sticks of wood on the dog-sled and told the two animals, "Now b'ys, take me home." With unerring instinct, the dogs, with Blizzard in the lead, had delivered George right to his door.

Now Blizzard was loose again. Skulking slowly up the road, the angry animal wagged his huge head from side to side, growling continuously as he surveyed his surroundings. It seemed to the people watching that he was trying to pick out his first victim. Nobody moved. Everybody watched from a safe distance, hoping that George Doyle would soon arrive to recapture the escaped animal. But Doyle was nowhere to be seen.

They were all surprised and more than a bit alarmed when a small figure stepped forward and started to walk slowly toward the menacing dog. Blizzard stopped in his tracks. With hackles raised, fangs bared, and great streams of saliva dripping from his mouth, he was obviously puzzled by the creature daring to approach him. Those watching saw young William Jackman draw near the dog and hesitate for a brief moment. Then, ignoring the warnings of the adults standing by, he continued on, crooning softly to the dog as he did so. Reaching in toward Blizzard's broad chest, he gingerly took hold of the short length of broken chain dangling from the animal's neck. The people, who only a few minutes earlier had pleaded with him to turn back and still feared for his safety, watched in amazement as the big dog permitted himself to be led back toward the store from which he had escaped. Doyle, finally arriving on the scene, was vastly relieved to see Blizzard in the custody of the young boy. Within minutes the huge dog was once again back on his chains.

Catherine was deeply shaken by the incident. That night she chided William for the great risk he had taken. Sleepily he replied, "Don't worry about me, Mother. Sure, whenever I give Sailor a few pats, I always pats poor old Blizzard too. Nobody except me seems to like him very much. And I think he likes me a little bit too. Sometimes he licks my hand when I give him a few caplin."

With that William turned into his pillow and, within seconds, was fast asleep. Catherine stayed, looked at him for several long minutes, once again offered a short prayer of thanks for having delivered her son from harm that day, and marvelled at the young hero now snoring blissfully in the bed.

As stalwart and forthright as he was, however, William was no angel. Like all children of his age, he got into his fair share of trouble and mischief. His mother swore that he "never knew what a door or a gate was for." He left the gate to the chicken coop open so many times that Catherine, tired of chasing her few hens all over Renews, finally stopped asking him to check to see if there were any eggs and took that daily chore upon herself.

William was long accustomed to the frequent scoldings that Catherine delivered whenever he committed some small transgression. His normal reaction was one of immediate repentance. Mother and son would then hug each other and the issue of the moment would be quickly forgotten. One day, however, something in his mother's rebuke stung him, and instead of responding in the usual manner, he stormed from the house crying, "You'll be sorry. You'll see." As he fled from the house, his eyes strayed to the large puncheon that his father had recently placed in the far corner of the yard to be used later for barking fishing twine. Almost without thinking, he ran to the puncheon and lowered himself into it, ignoring the sticky residue of the molasses that had been its original contents. Hunkered down, he was able to keep track of whatever was happening by peering through the bung-hole or by occasionally popping his head up for a quick look around. He stayed there all morning. Around noon Catherine wondered briefly why William had not yet appeared for his midday meal, but assumed that he was off somewhere on one of his sojourns. As the afternoon wore on, however, she grew a little uneasy and asked some of the other children if they had seen her son anywhere. By suppertime she was really worried and walked all around the community looking for him. William, cramped and now hungry, but determined to punish his mother to the fullest extent, remained in his hiding place in the puncheon. He was also by now a little bit concerned about what would happen to him when he was eventually discovered.

By dusk Catherine was panic-stricken, certain by now that some serious mishap had overtaken her son. She imagined him lying bleeding or dead at the bottom of some cliff or drowned in the salt water off Renews. She pleaded with the men and women of nearby houses to help her search for him, which they did, but to no avail. Crying uncontrollably and praying constantly to the Blessed Virgin Mary and Saint Jude, the patron saint of lost causes, she called her son's name over and over into the near darkness.

Finally William could resist no longer. From his hiding place, he called, "Yoohoo, I'm over here." His mother, thinking she had heard something, but not quite sure, listened again. Once more came the cry, "Yoohoo, I'm over here." Following the sound, Catherine soon found him in the barrel. For several seconds she did not know whether to throttle him or to hold him. Then her motherly instincts won out and still crying, she pressed her errant son to her trembling body. He hugged and kissed her in return, and all was forgiven.

That same fall, Thomas, on one of his last trips home for the year, brought back with him a few special things that were to be saved for Christmas, just a few short weeks away. The precious items included a box of the popular cookies known everywhere as *thousands and millions*. Literally covered with hundreds of minute pieces of multicoloured confection, these tasty tidbits had long been a regular Christmas treat for the Jackman family. The box was placed in the coolness of the outside pantry where the rest of the family's food reserves were kept.

In the days that followed, William often thought about the cookies sitting just a few feet away, especially whenever he felt a bit hungry. Finally, he succumbed to the temptation to take one, convincing himself that nobody would miss a cookie or two. But he did not stop there. Each day his sense of guilt would be pushed aside by his insatiable craving for another of the dainty morsels. He sneaked another, and another . . . then sometimes three or four in the same day.

When Christmas arrived, to the shock and dismay of the rest of the family, the box was practically empty. Only a handful of broken cookie fragments lay on the bottom. Michael and James cried with disappointment. Infant Arthur was still too young to care. Shamefaced, William sheepishly admitted to being the culprit. Catherine, in her usual way, lectured him for several long minutes on the evils of greed and gluttony. William stood and took the verbal punishment that he so well deserved. It was his father's stony silence, however, that stung William much more than his mother's tirade and far more than any slap or body blow could have ever done. He knew that he had disappointed the man that he admired and loved above all others. He vowed to himself that he would never again do anything to earn his father's disfavour.

During the winter of 1849, as William approached his thirteenth birthday, Thomas and Catherine decided that their son was now old enough to go to work. Although they would have preferred that William go to Labrador with Thomas on the *Fanny Bloomer*, they both agreed that it might be better if William stayed closer to home where he could help his mother while his father was away, and finish the last of his schooling. William himself, with the independent spirit that was already clearly evident in him, told them both that he too wouldn't mind getting on with another crew and trying it without his father's help. So arrangements were made to have him join another schooner, the *Marian*, later in the spring after the *Fanny Bloomer* had left for Labrador. The vessel, owned and operated by Captain Eric Ryan of Trepassey, a close friend of Thomas, was a small twenty-five-ton schooner. It was undersized for the long and sometimes dangerous voyages to Labrador or the Grand Banks, and usually fished the calmer waters of St. Mary's Bay and Placentia Bay. This would have the added advantage of allowing William to return home several times during the summer. Both parents felt that a summer on the *Marian* would be a good start for him. Thomas knew that his son would eventually join him on the *Fanny Bloomer*, but there was lots of time for that yet. He thought that a summer or two of fishing with someone else might harden and prepare William for the life's work ahead of him.

The winter passed slowly. With the approach of spring, William began to look forward to his first real fishing voyage. He and his mother spent many hours putting together the kitbag that he would need to take with him. He was ready to go whenever he got the call.

Before his departure, however, an unforeseen sequence of events would unfold that would not only delay William's entry into the codfishery until the following year, but would change his life forever.

The first significant event of that momentous spring and summer occurred in mid-April. The winter had been uncharacteristically mild, and this day in particular was more like a day that one might expect in June or July. The last of the winter's ice and snow had melted a few weeks earlier, and the men of the community, encouraged by such an early spring, prepared to get a head start on the new fishing season ahead.

Just three days before the *Marian* was set to leave for the fishing grounds of Placentia Bay, William was at his usual place on the wharf. John Power, the tall, thin boy that William considered to be his best friend, sat next to him, his legs, like William's, dangling over the edge.

"Well, Will b'y, only another couple of days and you're gone off for the summer. I wish I was going with you. I'll just be stuck here helping me fadder again, I s'pose."

"Yes b'y, it won't be long now, will it?"

But John's words had stirred in William a strange and conflicting mixture of emotions. He was indeed looking forward to going. At the same time he knew instinctively that once he set foot on board the *Marian* into the world of men, the games and pastimes of his childhood would be over, at least for the few months away from home. He realized that this might, in fact, be one of the very last days that he would ever spend connoring with John and the other boys. He knew that he would most likely be gone all summer and most of the fall. Besides connoring, he would miss the trouting, swimming, and many other boyhood activities that had always filled his days, even mass, and the few hours that he spent in school on most days. He would also miss the long walks over the barrens of Renews in search of the blueberries and partridge-berries that he loved so much.

The thought of berry-picking brought to his mind the left-over partridgeberries that sometimes survive the winter and are still there in the spring when the ice and snow has melted.

"John, you know what I think we should do? Let's give this up and go in to see if there's any "spring berries" this year. What do you say?"

"Yes b'y, that's a grand idea. I'll come. Sure, me mouth is just watering with the thought of it."

As they discussed their plans, their conversation was over-heard by two young girls playing nearby. The words were scarcely spoken before the bigger and older of the two girls, Mary Ryan, scrambled to her feet and interrupted the boys.

"Me and Annie are coming too. I don't care what you says."

William tried to discourage the girl, telling her that he and John intended to go alone.

"Besides, Annie can't go anyway. I know her mother wouldn't let her."

"Will Jackman, if you don't take us, we'll just follow you any-way. And then if anything happens to us, you'll be to blame for it."

Before William could say anything more, Mary darted off, only to return a few minutes later to tell the boys, "Annie can so go. Her mother said it was okay as long as William was looking after her and she didn't go too far. Or stay too long."

William, feeling trapped, turned to John for support. But John simply shrugged his shoulders in a gesture of resignation and said, "Sure I s'pose it's alright for them to come. I don't think they'll be too much trouble."

Within minutes, the little group of would-be berry pickers set out on the twenty-five minute walk to the berry grounds. Following the footpath through the barrens that he had travelled many times before, William enjoyed the feel of the warm sun on his neck and shoulders. He hoped that there would be a few berries waiting to reward them for their efforts.

Partridgeberries grow in abundance on the barrens and hills of the Southern Shore, usually ripening by the end of August or early September. During the long winter months, jams, jellies, pies, and puddings made from these tart, tangy berries would make a welcome diversion from the otherwise bland and unvaried diet of many families. With the first frosts of late fall or early winter, most of the berries fall to the ground, composting the area around them for another year. Each year a few berries, however, would somehow manage to cling to the low-lying plants on which they grew. Encased in a cover of ice and snow, some of these tenacious survivors would then make it through the winter. In the spring they would be transformed into a fruit of such rare succulence that many of the residents of the nearby communities would often walk miles just to get a handful of the coveted delicacies. Spring berries, however, could never be picked in any great quantity; a handful or a cupful was the most for which anyone could ever hope. Still, every year, the first few fine days of spring would bring these treasured morsels to the minds of many people.

Skipping along holding William's hand, Annie was enjoying herself too. Every now and then William would invite her to ride on his shoulders, but she would only stay there for a few minutes and then demand to be put down again. She didn't want to miss out on anything in what was for her a rare adventure. Annie was eleven years old, but her tiny frame gave her the appearance of a six or seven-year-old. She had been very ill from the moment that she was born. During the first year of her life, she had hovered continuously between life and death. The following year her parents had taken her to St. John's. The kindly doctor who examined her told them that one of the valves of their daughter's heart was not functioning at its full capacity. It was a condition that today can be corrected with minor surgery, but at that time there was nothing that could be done to effectively remedy her situation. The doctor said she might improve as she grew older, although he doubted it and told her parents to just take care of her as best they could. Her poor health was further compounded by the fact that she had very poor eyesight as well. Many of the things around her she simply saw as blurred shapes and shadows. Only very close up could she see things in any real detail. Despite her problems, however, she was a happy little girl and was known throughout the community for her singing and her ability to whistle. She knew all the songs of her time and often composed little tunes and ditties of her own that pleased and amused other children and adults alike. The feeling that William felt for Annie as he watched her skip along was one of pity, that she was unable to do many of the ordinary things that other children took for granted, tempered with admiration for the tiny girl who seemed so oblivious to her handicaps.

Mary Ryan, in contrast to Annie, was a strong, robust girl of thirteen. She was extremely loud and very outspoken. Constantly hungry, she immediately devoured every scrap of food that came her way. People often suspected her of stretching the truth, and although she was never caught in the act of stealing, things sometimes seemed to mysteriously disappear when she was around. Yet most people generally liked her for her carefree manner and her boundless energy. Now, as the small group walked along, she tried to keep ahead of the others, determined to be the first one to sample the juicy morsels that lay waiting.

John Power brought up the rear. Painfully thin, he walked with a slight limp, the result of a broken leg that hadn't been set properly three years earlier. From one of the poorest families in Renews, his ill-fitting and threadbare clothing offered little protection or comfort, and his young body suffered constantly from the damp, cold weather of the Southern Shore. Now, as he walked along, he kept an eye out for spots that looked promising enough for him to tail a few rabbit slips in the fall.

Because of Annie, it took the little group of berry-pickers almost thirty-five minutes to reach their destination. When they scattered to search for berries, William kept a watchful eye on the others to make sure nobody strayed out of sight. He didn't have to worry about Annie. She stayed very close to him all the time, following him like a shadow whenever he moved to a new spot. Her constant stream of questions and chatter told him where she was at every minute. It was Mary that he was mostly concerned about. He knew that she could wander off by herself without even realizing that she had done so.

The sought-after spring berries were very scarce, but by two o'clock their tins contained at least a few of the precious morsels . . . all except Mary's. Every berry that she picked was immediately popped into her mouth. Her fingers and face were discolored a dark red from the juices of the berries that she had consumed.

It was then that William noticed for the first time the heavy dark clouds that had drifted in to mar the previously clear, sunny sky. The air suddenly felt a little colder. He told himself that if it started to rain or got much colder, they might have to cut their berry-picking expedition short and head for home. Ten minutes later he noted that the wind had swung around and was now blowing from the north-east and that ominously blacker clouds now covered most of the already overcast sky.

Noting that Annie had suddenly ceased her chattering and seemed to be in some discomfort, he asked her if she was cold.

"Yes, Will, I'm freezing. I wish I had brought me coat along."

"That's okay, Annie, I think we'll go home now anyway."

Despite the protestations of the others, the little group soon set off on their trek back to the community.

Not more than a few minutes into their journey home, the first few snowflakes appeared. The children, with Annie perched almost weightlessly astride William's strong shoulders, quickened their pace. The wind continued to increase in strength, and the snow thickened by the minute. Then almost before they knew it, the children found themselves trapped in the midst of one of the worst spring blizzards that the Southern Shore had seen in many years.

Almost two miles from home and unable to see for more than a few feet in the blinding snow, William knew that they were in trouble. He was, at the tender age of twelve, forced to make a decision that would haunt him for the rest of his life: whether to continue on, or to seek some form of shelter in the hope that the storm would soon pass. He knew that in the white-out conditions of the storm they might stray off in the wrong direction and be even worse off than they already were. He doubted that he and the others, especially Annie, would last to make it all the way back home, clad only in their thin summer clothing. They might perish along the way. His instincts told him that they should take shelter as best they could and wait. Groping around in the swirling snow, he led the others to a small thicket of low-lying alders where they all huddled together in the pitifully scant protection that the scrawny trees afforded.

Freezing and terrified, they waited, trying to take some warmth and comfort in the closeness of each others' bodies. Each passing minute seemed like an eternity. The storm raged on. Then darkness fell. Numbed with cold, William and John tried to pack some of the fallen snow around them, but most of it blew away as soon as they scooped it in place. They waited...and waited. Sometimes they talked in low voices to reassure themselves that everything would soon be alright again.

William tried his best to comfort the others, especially Mary and Annie, by telling them that he was sure that by now someone from the community was certainly out looking for them and would soon be here. He held his arms around Annie as she snuggled as tightly as possible against his chest. He felt her tiny body shivering violently as she hugged him. He wished that he could give her some of his own clothing but he, like the others, had on only his thin summer clothing. Whenever he felt her slipping off into sleep or unconsciousness, he prodded her awake and talked to her to make sure she didn't drop off again. He knew that with her frail body and weak heart, she was more vulnerable than the rest of them to the cold, biting wind and snow that battered them, and feared that if she drifted off she might never wake again. He realized that he must keep them all awake and as alert as possible at all times.

Suddenly, without warning, Mary scrambled to her feet. Screaming incoherently, she bolted off into the darkness. Startled and stunned by this unexpected turn of events, William didn't know what to do. He knew that if he tried to follow her he would have no way of knowing where she went in the darkness and that he might never find his way back to the others again. The sense of responsibility that he suddenly felt for the welfare of the other two, especially Annie, told him that their only hope of survival was to stay where they were. He was forced to make another gut-wrenching decision. He stayed.

Back in Renews, it was almost dark before the alarm went out that the children were missing. Within a matter of minutes, a group of men formed themselves into a search party and set out towards the barrens in the direction that they thought the children had taken. Carrying oil lanterns, they plodded along in single file, each man careful to keep the man in front of him in view, even though the distance that separated them was only a few short feet. They took with them George Doyle's Sailor and another dog belonging to Mary's father to help them locate the missing children and, if need be, to help they themselves find their own way back home again in the storm.

Twenty-five or thirty minutes into their trek, the men, now freezing and wet themselves, reasoned that they must be nearing the berry site. They called the names of the missing children continuously into the night, but the sound of their voices carried only a short distance on the howling wind. They crept on. Precious minutes passed, then a half-hour. An hour later they were still searching, even unsure themselves now of exactly where they were.

They were at the point of despairing that they might never find the children in time, when Sailor suddenly stopped and held his massive head to the side as if listening to some distant sound, growling deeply in his throat as he did so. Sensing that they might finally be in the vicinity of the children, the men renewed their shouting as loudly and as continuously as they could. They tried to call out in unison to make the sound of their combined voices carry as far as possible in the wind. It was several minutes before a faint answering call came out of the darkness of the night. Shortly after, they stumbled upon the three frightened children still clinging to each other in their pitiful shelter.

When told about Mary, three of the men broke off from the rest of the group and went in search of the still missing girl. They had gone only a short distance when one of the men saw what he thought might be a faint trail in the snow that had somehow not yet been eradicated by the shifting wind and swirling snow. Following it with great difficulty in the poor light of their lanterns, they were led to the very edge of one of the many ponds that dotted the barrens and woods in the area. There the faint pattern in the snow seemed to indicate footprints that had stopped and then turned off in another direction. Groping along, fearing that the already almost indiscernible trail might be totally obliterated at any minute, they were relieved to find Mary just a short while later. She was huddled in the shelter of a very large boulder, with her head resting against the side of the snow-covered rock. To their astonishment, however, the girl, wild-eyed and raving, fled once more into the night as they approached. It would be several more minutes before they were able to find her again.

When they got back to the others, they found that some of the men had managed to get a fire started. They knew that they had to get the children and themselves thawed out and revived before they could attempt the difficult journey back. William felt strangely detached as he watched the surrealistic scene before him. Across the flickering flames of the fire, against the backdrop of the swirling darkness, he watched as John and Mary, like himself, huddled as close as possible to the warmth of the blaze. Both were now covered in the blankets and extra clothing that the men had brought with them. Edmund Ryan held Annie in his arms, using the great bulk of his body to protect his daughter as best he could from the storm. They all sat there, trying to coax life back into their frozen bodies.

The scene was hushed. Nobody spoke. They were all, for the moment, lost in their own thoughts. It was several minutes before they realized that the strange sound that they heard in the wind was the quiet sobbing of Edmund Ryan.

"Oh my God! My God! She's gone! She's gone!", the big man moaned over and over, as he clutched his young daughter tightly to his chest. It was a while before the others finally realized that the tiny girl with the bad heart had succumbed to her ordeal as she lay in her father's arms and had quietly slipped away into eternity.

The sad procession of men and children that finally made its way back to the community was met by other men and women waiting in readiness in the parish hall. A roaring fire warmed the large room, and pots of steaming water stood on the stove. Stripped of their frozen clothing, the children were quickly wrapped in warm blankets and fed bowls of scalding tea and hot soup. They had their hands, feet, and ears rubbed vigorously to remove the whiteness of the frostbite that still threatened their extremities. Everyone watched in hushed silence as the parish priest said the last rites over the still body of Annie Ryan, now lying on one of the hall's long tables, surrounded by her family and others who stood around in shock and disbelief. As he felt the sweet warmth flow through his body, William felt himself drifting off to sleep. Everything seemed totally unreal to him and his mind still hadn't accepted the reality of Annie's death.

Annie was buried three days later. Her funeral was one of the saddest ever to be held on the Southern Shore. People everywhere mourned the death of the little girl who had battled so hard for eleven years, only to die in a freak spring blizzard on the bleak barrens of Renews. Later that spring, a man travelling along the footpath that passed by the site of the tragedy, spotted a small leather shoe lying half-buried in the goudie[7] and bog laurel. He picked it up and placed it on a nearby rock. For years after, travellers passing through the area would see the worn shoe, bless themselves, and sometimes murmur a quick prayer. They all recognized the tiny and by now moss-covered shoe as a monument to the little girl who had perished in that hallowed spot on that fateful night in April.

Apart from slight frostburn, John emerged from his ordeal relatively unscathed, at least outwardly. Whether it was his extremely painful shyness or some unconscious desire to suppress it from his memory, he did not want to talk about the incident. He answered questions with mere grunts or a slight shake or nod of his head or, at best, an occasional monosyllabic yes or no. After a while, people stopped asking him. Despite the gauntness of his appearance and his constant state of near starvation, however, he had survived. In fact, he would continue to live, although bent and arthritic in his later years, to the ripe age of seventy-nine, raising eight children in the process. One of his grandsons would one day take his place as an able lieutenant in the Responsible Government of Sir Robert Bond, the first of a long line of Powers to offer themselves to Newfoundland's political arena.

Unlike John, it took Mary three days to come to her senses. When she did, she wanted to talk continuously about her experience. She revelled in the attention suddenly focused upon her. When one of her rescuers commented on how she had nearly walked straight into the pond, she silenced them all when she told them, "I was so frightened, I was just runnin' away. I didn't know where I was. I couldn't even see where I was going. Then someone took me by the arm and led me away to that place where you found me. I can't remember anything else after that."

Mary would never be a deeply religious woman. She swore to her dying day, however, that what she told the people that day was the gospel truth. She never once in her lifetime veered from her story.

The *Marian* sailed without William. His mother told him, "Never mind, my son, perhaps you'll get on with some other crew later on."

In the days and weeks that followed, William withdrew into himself. He experienced a despondency and sense of loss unlike anything he had ever felt before. He couldn't push the memory from his mind of little Annie dying in her father's arms. He agonized over and over about his decision to take shelter rather than to try to continue on towards home. The fact that he knew in his heart that he had done the only thing possible under the circumstances gave him no comfort. He would never forget the feelings of helplessness and despair that he had known that night on the barrens.

However, the first few warm days of June improved William's outlook a little. The anguish of Annie's death gradually softened into the bitter-sweet melancholy that acceptance and the passage of time brings. Catherine knew how her young son felt. With the innate wisdom of a mother, she tried to keep him busy, hoping that concentration on work might give him some respite from the innermost thoughts that were still obviously troubling his young mind.

He now spent more time with John than ever before. The two boys, having shared and survived the ordeal on the barrens, had grown much closer. Every day, as soon as they were free of their regular chores, they still did the usual things—connoring on the wharf, trouting, and swimming. But somehow everything was different now. Often they just roamed around the community, sometimes talking, at other times just walking along together in comfortable silence, each boy lost in his own thoughts.

The second incident that would make 1849 the most memorable year in William's life occurred on a nice warm Tuesday in the first week of July. On that day the boys' meandering took them to the top of a steep embankment a short distance from the community. Lying in the tall grass that overlooked the salt water below, they had taken off their shirts and were enjoying the feel of the warm sun on their bodies. They scanned the horizon for the sign of schooners and other vessels out on the water.

The lowing of the wind in the trees, the sound of the waves breaking softly on the beach below, and the gentle swaying of the grass around him had suddenly made William lethargic and drowsy. He felt himself dozing off. He was almost asleep when he heard John speak.

"Will, do you ever think about Annie?"

Surprised by the question, especially since it came from John, William took a moment before replying, "Yes b'y, I can't hardly tell you how much she's on my mind. There's not an hour nor a day goes by that I don't think about her. I'm sure I dream about her every night. What about you?"

"I do too. I don't think I'll ever get over it. The more I think about it the more I blame myself. I s'pose we shouldn't have took her with us."

It was a rare thing for the taciturn John to reveal his innermost thoughts in this manner. Even to William, his closest friend, he had never talked like this before. William, with his eyes still closed, waited for more. The words that he heard next, however, were not what he expected.

"Lard dyin', Wiil, look at that now, will you!"

William followed John's line of vision to the beach below. There he saw too the three eider ducks that John had just spotted. Swimming placidly in the water at the base of the cliff, forty feet below, the sight of the birds had instantly changed the melancholy of the moment into one now charged with excitement and anticipation.

"Oh b'ys, oh b'ys, oh b'ys. What I wouldn't give for a feed of one of them." Forever hungry, John's mouth watered at the thought of the taste of a juicy, tender salt-water duck for his supper.

Ducks like these, along with turrs, puffins and other seabirds, frequented the waters of the Southern Shore. Most fishermen, however, ignored them and chose instead to pursue the partridge that abounded on the surrounding barrens. John Power's father, Nicholas was an exception, and had been bringing home the occasional salt-water duck for as long as John could remember. John could never get enough of them, and often wondered why anyone would prefer the stringy, gamey taste of partridge over the rich, dark meat of any kind of sea bird, especially duck.

"We got to get them, Will, b'y. Come on."

Both boys jumped to their feet. Taking careful aim, they hurled fist-size rocks at the unsuspecting ducks below. They missed. At the sound of the first splash, the ducks took flight, and the disappointed boys watched them disappear into the distance.

"Maybe they'll come back."

The next day the boys returned to the same spot, hoping that the ducks had returned. Their pulses quickened when, sure enough, they again spotted the ducks swimming below, as if the events of the previous day had never taken place. The boys' second attempt to hit them with rocks, however, met with the same result as on the previous day. On Thursday, they tried again with no better result.

Frustrated in their efforts, the two boys were now drawn to the ducks like a magnet. They were obsessed with the thought of getting at least one of them. They had not yet given any thought to how they would retrieve them from the water when they finally killed them.

"I don't care, Will. I'm havin' one of them ducks s'posin' I got to come here every day this summer. And don't tell anyone else cause then they'll be after 'em too."

Early Friday morning the boys were back once more. And again their missiles fell short of the mark. As they stood there in frustration watching the ducks fly away yet again, John looked at William and said, "I think I knows a way we can get at 'em." He then proceeded to explain how they could lower themselves down the cliff on a length of rope to swat the unsuspecting victims from overhead with sticks. William scoffed at the suggestion, but then, as he thought a bit further about it, allowed that it might be worth a try. That very afternoon they again returned to the cliff, this time armed with a long length of rope and a couple of stout clubs chosen from the Jackmans' woodpile.

William volunteered to be the first to go down. Having fastened one end of the rope around the bole of a nearby spruce tree, he started to loop the other end around his waist. John, momentarily preoccupied with checking to see if the ducks were still there, was startled to hear his friend's sudden shriek of panic. He spun around in time to see William teetering at the very edge of the embankment, his arms flailing wildly as he tried to regain his balance while the overhang crumbled away beneath his feet. John watched in horror as William tumbled head-over-heels down the sharp incline. He saw his friend's body somersault through the air as it met an outcropping halfway down, to finally come to rest at the base of the cliff, half in and half out of the water. John's first impulse was to try to climb down himself, but for some reason that he could never afterwards explain, he instead turned and ran as fast as he could back toward the community to get help.

When John returned twenty-five minutes later with a small group of rescuers, two of the men were lowered down the embankment where they found William unconscious and bleeding profusely. Immediately they knew that he was seriously injured, perhaps even beyond help. Had it been a sheer drop, the fall would have undoubtedly killed him instantly. Even so, the embankment had been too steep for him to arrest or check his descent, and the hundreds of sharp rocks and small trees and shrubs that jutted out of the seventy-degree incline had punished his body mercilessly as he tumbled down. Only the fact that he had he landed with his head facing inward toward the embankment had prevented him from drowning before they reached him.

As gently as they could, the men carried him home. News of William's fall preceded his arrival. His mother, along with Aunt Maggie and her great supply of bandages, salves, and ointments, was waiting for him. Even though they had been warned about William's condition, they were still not quite prepared for the sight that met them. Both women wept openly when they saw the dozens of cuts and bruises that covered the young boy's entire body. They worked feverishly to staunch the bleeding, dressing and bandaging his wounds as best they could. Their initial examination told them that he did not, miraculously, appear to have any broken bones. Later they would discover that, in fact, two of his fingers, a toe, and at least two of his ribs had been broken in the fall.

As he lay naked and bandaged on his bed, either Catherine or Aunt Maggie stayed constantly at his side. William's continuous moaning told them the extent of his suffering, and the herbal mixture that Aunt Maggie gave him did little to alleviate his pain. He remained unconscious through the night.

The next morning, as Catherine and Aunt Maggie were trying to change his dressings, taking great care to be as gentle as possible, William finally awoke. Their efforts to get some water and a little warm broth into him met with little success. The slightest movement or even the merest touch on any part of his battered body caused him to scream in great agony. For the rest of the day he drifted in and out of consciousness.

On the morning of the third day, when Catherine and Aunt Maggie again examined his body, they were both alarmed to see the dark ugly redness that now circled many of William's wounds. Even more frightening were the tiny red lines that radiated from some of them. It was obvious to the two women that William was also by now running an extremely high fever. The cold, wet cloths placed upon his forehead and body seemed to do little to alleviate his obvious distress. By four o'clock that afternoon, both women noted that the condition of William's wounds had deteriorated even further in the space of a few short hours.

He babbled incoherently in a state of delirium, which told Aunt Maggie that the boy was now in grave danger. As she dressed his wounds once more, applying the salves and ointments that she had used to successfully treat so many people in the past, she prayed continually, knowing that now they could only wait . . . and hope.

The three past days had taken their toll on Catherine. The anguish that she felt for her son's suffering and the lack of rest had sapped her strength and concentration. Her mind was muddled and confused. She couldn't sleep. She couldn't eat. She agonized endlessly over the fact that Thomas, somewhere out on the salt water, was not even aware of his son's plight. She wished that he were here now to help her carry this great burden.

Aunt Maggie finally confided to her, "Catherine, my love, I got to tell you that nothing I'm doing seems to be doing any good. I don't know what else to do. I don't think there's anything more I can do for him," Catherine simply cried softy. She herself had already come to the realization that she might lose her first-born son even before the old woman had spoken these words.

They waited at William's bedside and prayed. Sometime in the wee hours of the morning Aunt Maggie drifted off to sleep. Like Catherine, she too had gone more hours than she cared to count without sleeping. An hour later, however, she awoke abruptly and sat bolt upright in her chair, suddenly wide awake. For several minutes she just sat there, lost in her thoughts. When Catherine, still awake and now sensing something in the older woman's actions, questioned her, Aunt Maggie told her, "Catherine, my dear, listen, I don't know what it means, but I just dreamt about Ernest Smyth. I never dreamt about him ever before in my life. I never even met the man. I only heard about him. It's the strangest thing. Maybe it's a token that he might be able to do something for William."

Patrick Connolly, next door, was a light sleeper. The loud rapping on his door brought him instantly awake.

From the top of his stairs he shouted down to whoever was outside, "In the name of the Blessed Virgin, who's there at this ungodly hour? What do ye want?"

"Paddy, open up. It's me, Catherine. I got to talk to you."

A minute later, clad only in long underwear that was in great need of a good washing, he opened his door to the obviously distressed woman waiting outside.

"What's wrong, my dear? Is it William? Sure 'tis only two o'clock."

"Paddy, I got to ask you and Michael to do something for me that I know I got no right to ask. But I don't know where else to turn. I need you to go to Ferryland and get Ernest Smyth for me."

The Connolly brothers lived together in the drafty old two-storey house that stood between the Jackman's house and the community schoolhouse at the top of the hill. It was one of the worst kept houses in the settlement. Most people viewed the Connollys as lazy and shiftless. They were the "hangashores" that every community had at least one or two of. Although they owned a small punt, they rarely ventured out on the water and were seldom known to do any kind of hard work. Yet, year after year, they somehow managed to survive. Nobody knew how they did it, for the brothers never asked much of the others in the community. Their needs must have been simple indeed.

Despite their slovenly ways, however, the brothers had always been good to Catherine and her young family. On many occasions they had helped her with some task or small emergency when Thomas was away at sea. It was comforting to her to know that they were there if she needed them. Now she was asking them to help her again, this time to undertake a mission of mercy that they might not be capable of performing.

Ferryland was a long distance away. Both men, now in their late fifties and far from being fit and healthy, knew that neither of them was up to the twenty-four-mile walk that the trip to Ferryland and back would entail.

Catherine was desperate. If the Connollys couldn't or wouldn't go, she would ask someone else. If all else failed, she would go herself.

"Perhaps you could take Thomas' skiff. Or I could ask Jim Murphy for the loan of his horse and cart. Whatever you think might be best."

The brothers discussed the matter between themselves for several minutes. If they possibly could, they wanted to help the young mother that they both liked so well and were also cognizant of the fact that the life of her son might be hanging in the balance. They reasoned that Murphy's horse might conceivably get one of them, possibly both, to Ferryland, as neither of them was very heavy. But there was no way that the animal, as big and strong as it was, would be able to pull both them and the great bulk of Smyth's two-hundred-and-fifty-pound body back to Renews. One of them would have to walk or stay behind in Ferryland.

In the end they chose the skiff. They left in the half-light of pre-dawn. The first half of the journey would be the hardest. With only the skiff's jib to assist them, they would have to tack the whole distance against the moderate north-east headwind that blew in from the Atlantic, hoping that they wouldn't have to do very much rowing. Unless the wind changed around or died down altogether, however, their return journey should be much easier— a fair, trailing wind bringing them home quickly. Eight hours later they were back, with the willing Smyth in tow.

Ernest Smyth was that rarest of creatures, the seventh son of a seventh son. Said to have been born with the power to heal, he was well-known along the entire length of the Southern Shore for his ministrations to the sick and the injured. He could stop hiccups by simply looking into a person's eyes for a few seconds. Warts disappeared within a fortnight after he had rubbed them with his huge hands and intoned incantations. People believed that he could cure many ailments with just the touch of his hands. Still, he was also known for his dark side. In truth, some people were somewhat afraid of him and believed that he could also impose curses and were therefore careful never to cross or offend him. Even animals seemed to sense his extraordinary powers and sometimes acted strangely when he was around. One man from the shore swore that he was present once when Smyth had demonstrated how he could make an earthworm, when placed upon his open palm, curl up, wither and die within minutes. For the most part, however, he was known for the many times that he had pulled some man, woman or child back from near death. When called upon, regardless of the hour, night or day, he was always ready and available.

Now, as he looked at William for the first time, Smyth shook his head sadly. He told Aunt Maggie, in a moment when Catherine was out of earshot, "I think that's the worse state I ever seen on a human body. I'm not sure I can do anything for him either. I knows he can't last much longer like this, though, perhaps only a few days . . . maybe not even that long."

He wanted to know what remedies Aunt Maggie had tried, knowing even before he asked that she would have almost certainly used the same ointments, salves, and treatments that he himself would have employed. They changed his dressings again.

And watched and waited. By now Catherine had lost all track of time. Everything was a blur. She hardly slept, and her usual serene appearance had taken on the gaunt and haunted look of a person deeply troubled. She moved about in a trance. She scarcely heard Smyth when he asked her, "Catherine, do you think I could have a drop of tea and a bite to eat? I haven't had a thing in me stomach since early this morning."

It was while he was sitting at the kitchen table, eating the food that Catherine brought him, that Smyth came up with the idea that would, in the end, save William's life.

"Look, there's just too many cuts and sores on your poor b'y's body for his system to fight 'em all off. He can't last much longer in that state. I don't think he could survive a trip in to St. John's either. They probably couldn't do anything for him by now anyway. The only hope would be if we could somehow keep him covered in some sort of healing solution. And there's only one thing like that I can think of around here—that's the salt water. The shock might kill him, I don't know. But there's nothing else left. He's going to die anyway if we don't do something." Catherine and Maggie looked at him aghast.

In disbelief, Catherine could hardly fathom Smyth's words. But Aunt Maggie, although startled herself at first by the man's suggestion, saw the possibility of Smyth's proposal, and it was she who finally convinced the distraught mother to agree to go ahead with it.

From the corner of the back porch they pulled out the cut-off barrel that the Jackmans, like many other families in the community, used when they washed their bodies. Small children could sit in the half-barrel and have at least the lower parts of their bodies completely covered by the bath water. Adults and older boys and girls, however, usually just stood up and poured jugs of hot water over themselves to cleanse and rinse their soaped-over bodies.

Smyth saw right away that it wouldn't serve the purpose.

"We needs something bigger . . . something that he can stretch out in so that his whole body is in the water, right up to his neck."

Their search turned up nothing better.

Smyth growled, "Even a coffin would do. If I had some boards I might be able to knock together something meself, even though I'm not much of a hand with a hammer and saw."

A few minutes later the Connolly brothers were approached by Catherine for the second time. She wanted them to build a bath-tub for her. The obliging brothers scrounged around for the wood that they needed, finding some among the jumble of objects that had been poked in around shores of the Jackman house and their own over the years. The rest they got by stripping boards off the side of their house that faced toward the school—less notice-able to the rest of the community. They could put most of them back again later. Under Smyth's watchful eye, the brothers quick-ly assembled the crude tub, chinked it with oakum rummaged from one of the nearby stages, and dragged it into the back porch of the Jackman house.

It took almost half an hour for the Connollys and the others to bring enough salt water from the beach to fill the long narrow box. Smyth advised against heating the water. He was concerned that it might lose some of its hoped-for healing properties in the process. Instead they waited another two hours for the water to lose some of its initial icy bite.

Catherine was numbed with the fear that her son might die in this last-ditch attempt to save him. She watched as the Connollys, one on either side of him, carried the semi-conscious boy as gently as they could to the tub. They paused, looking at Smyth for guidance. He nodded, and they started to slowly lower the prostrate boy into the water. When the cold, briny water met the cuts and sores on his body, William's body jerked spasmodical-ly. He screamed in extreme agony. And then he fainted. When the brothers started to lift him out again, Catherine stopped them. Summoning up more courage than she ever would again at any time in her life, she ordered them to "Put him back. Ernest says it must be at least fifteen minutes, and that is what it will be." It was the longest and most torturous fifteen minutes that she would ever know. William opened his eyes for a few seconds but was obviously unaware of what was happening to him.

That afternoon when they examined William again, his condition showed no improvement. However, to the practiced eye of Smyth and Aunt Maggie, the sores did not seem to have gotten any worse. With renewed hope, however faint, the three of them again sat and watched through the night. The next day was a repetition of the first. William again fainted, and Catherine again, with a will of steel that she didn't know she possessed, held him there for the prescribed amount of time. His wounds still showed little or no improvement, but as before, there did not appear to have been any further deterioration. On the third day, William remained conscious for most of the fifteen minutes that he spent in the water, although he moaned and babbled continuously for most of the time that he was there. This time, when they examined him, they were certain that the redness of the sores and the lines that radiated from them had finally abated somewhat.

William's recovery from that point was rapid. His fever broke. For the next five days the daily treatment in the back porch was repeated. Dozens of buckets of additional salt water were fetched from the beach to replenish and replace the water in the tub.

On the sixth day, William told them that he wasn't getting into the tub anymore. Instead, he said, he would go down to the beach himself and simply walk out into the water. His mother argued and protested until Smyth ventured his opinion that what William was proposing might in fact be better and save them all a lot of extra work in the bargain.

Ernest Smyth returned to Ferryland. Before he left, he told them that William must continue his daily immersions for at least another month to make sure that the poisons that had ravaged his body and threatened his life were completely exorcized.

Catherine made a third visit to the Connolly brothers, this time to bring them freshly baked bread and a jar of her rhubarb jam. Before leaving, she planted a grateful kiss on each of their stubbled faces, which pleased the scruffy old bachelors as much as if they had just been handed a fistful of gold coins.

William went to the beach every day without fail for his treatment. Sometimes John Power accompanied him, although he never once got into the cold water himself.

Although he still looked haggard and thin from his ordeal, William felt his strength returning. His body had by now become more acclimatized to the iciness of the salt water. He learned by experimentation that the sudden shock of a quick plunge was preferable to the agony of slow immersion, and on most days he would simply walk out a few feet, brace himself for a second or two, and duck under. Sometimes he even swam a a few strokes to help pass the time.

The cuts and sores on his body gradually healed, and the scabs that had covered his body finally dried up and fell off. For a few days, the terrible itching that accompanied the healing process was almost as bad as the pain he had felt earlier. It nearly drove him insane, especially during the nights. Aunt Maggie, who still came every day to check on his progress, sometimes bandaged his hands before he went to bed so that he wouldn't tear his wounds open again as he slept. Even in the daytime, the constant itching caused him great discomfort. Aunt Maggie's ointment helped a little, but the only thing that offered any real relief was the time he spent immersed in the salt water. Whenever the itching became too unbearable, he found himself going to the beach, not just once, but sometimes two or three times in the same day.

By the time Ernest Smyth's prescribed month was up, William's body had almost completely healed, although many of the scars would mar him forever. He had regained most of the weight that he had lost and his strength was almost back to normal. Still, William did not cut out his daily visits to the beach. He continued to swim every day, going further and further each time. Like many of today's runners and physical-fitness addicts, he was now obsessed with the daily routine.

By the end of August he was able to swim out to the furthest of the many semi-submerged rocks that dotted the Renews harbour or back and forth across the harbour several times. The little children who sometimes came to watch him would often ask him to take them for a ride on his back. When he did so, carrying them for a short distance close to shore, he got as much enjoyment out of the event himself as the squealing youngster that was getting the "free ride."

William swam until late September, when the water became too cold. By then, the frenzied thrashing movements that had characterized his earlier attempts at swimming were replaced by a powerful breast-stroke that enabled him to swim effortlessly for hours on end. In time, he would become, arguably, the strongest swimmer that Newfoundland has ever known. It would be his life-long passion. For years after, men would watch in amusement and admiration as William, at some point in the day, would strip, dive overboard, and swim alongside their schooner, easily keeping up with the vessel as she moved through the water.

The final and perhaps most profound event of those momentous few months occurred in late October. Almost fully recovered now from his fall, he accompanied his father and a couple of other men on a one-day trip to Trepassey. The *Dolphin* left Renews before first light and arrived in Trepassey a few hours later. By mid-morning the vessel's cargo had been unloaded and the schooner reloaded for its return trip back to Renews. Just as they were ready to leave, a young boy came looking for Thomas, to tell him that a Mr. Burbridge wanted to see him. With William in tow, Thomas set off to visit his old friend whom he had intended to drop in on anyway before they left.

As he waited, his father and Samuel Burbridge talked about many things, mostly the small talk of two friends who had known each other for a long time. He admired the fine furniture and paintings that decorated the large room in which they were seated. At mid-afternoon they were served tea and biscuits, brought in by a pretty, fair-haired girl, who smiled shyly at William and his father as she poured their tea. William had no way of knowing then that he had just met, for the first time, the girl who would eventually become his wife.

Even though Bridget Burbridge was only twelve years old, she carried herself with the poise and dignity of a woman. She was, in fact, the woman of the house. Her mother had died when Bridget was eight years old, and the young girl had kept house for her father and herself since that time. She couldn't remember her arrival in Newfoundland ten years earlier when her parents, both from Lancashire, England, had decided to try their luck in the New World. They had lived in St. John's for the first several years of their stay in Newfoundland, but Samuel, after the death of his wife, had accepted a position as agent for Bowring Brothers in Trepassey.

William would gladly have stayed in Trepassey overnight, but Thomas was anxious to clear land before nightfall. Even so, it was dark by the time the *Dolphin* cleared Mistaken Point. William stood with his father at the wheel, enjoying the feel of the salty air on his face. He felt much better than he had in months.

William was watching the light on Cape Race when Thomas turned to him and said, "Here, Will, you take her. Just keep the Southern Star on your left shoulder. Call me when we gets to Renews Head. I'm going below for a spell with the b'ys."

With that he was gone. Surprised and bewildered, William tried to fight back the panic that he felt rise within him. His first reaction was to call his father back. But something inside stopped him and, gripping the wheel determinedly with both hands, he instead tried to peer into the darkness ahead. The night was cold and clear, and the outline of the shore and the cliffs was clearly visible in the moonlight as they glided past. Gradually, as he listened to the whisper of the wind in the sails and the sound of the waves slapping gently against the bow of the schooner as she ploughed through the calm water, he began to relax.

Suddenly he felt more alive than ever before in his life. He knew at that instant that this was what he wanted to do forever. He had always realized that he would probably spend most of his life on the water, but now he knew beyond all doubt. The exhilaration that he felt at that time would resurface many times over in the coming years, and his deep love of the sea would never diminish. It was his life's calling.

When the stark outline of Renews Head finally came into view, William reluctantly turned the wheel back to his father.

Thomas merely nodded at his son and said, "Okay, b'y, I'll take her in." The surge of love that William felt for his father at that moment was something that he would remember and cherish for the rest of his life.

They That Go Down To the Sea in Ships

LET ME FEEL MY DORY LIFT
TO THE BROAD ATLANTIC COMBERS,
WHERE THE TIDE RIPS SWIRL
AND THE WILD DUCKS WHIRL
WHERE OLD NEPTUNE CALLS THE NUMBERS
'NEATH THE BROAD ATLANTIC COMBERS

— "Let Me Fish Off Cape St. Mary's"
Otto P. Kelland

The two men faced each other across the splitting table. The frozen grimace of the older man showed the decay of his gums and the tobacco stains on his teeth. His eyes bulged, and his laboured breath came in sharp wheezes and short gasps. The veins that stood out on his temples and neck threatened to burst at any minute. Droplets of sweat fell from his forehead to the surface of the table below.

The younger man stared impassively at him across the table. Then, despite the contortions of his much heavier opponent, he slowly and effortlessly pushed the arm of the other man down to the table and held it there for a second or two. Although the onlookers had all seen it many times before, they still hooted with amusement and glee at the scene they had just witnessed.

"Now b'ys, that's enough. We haven't got time for this kind of foolishness. We got work to do." Thomas Jackman, who had stood unnoticed in the background while the contest was taking place, had seen it all before too. Even so, he had still enjoyed seeing yet another exhibition of his son's great strength as much as any man there.

Gracious in defeat, the older man clapped William on the back. "By the Lard Reevin', Will, me son, there's not many around here that can do that to Ike Johnson . . . and I've had me go at the best of 'em, I can tell you."

At nineteen, William was already one of the strongest men on the Southern Shore. His massive neck and big hands and forearms were ample evidence of the great physical strength he possessed. But the most telling feature of his powerful body was his shoulders, muscled and broadened by the hard work that he did every day and by the hundreds of hours that he had spent swimming in the salt water in the last six years. Standing a hair under six feet, the hundred and ninety-five pounds that he carried on his frame were pure muscle, with scarcely an ounce of excess fat. It was well-known up and down the shore that William could single- handedly lift a full barrel of fish from the wharf to the schooner or vice versa. The work of other men would often be interrupted when they stopped to watch William carry or lift some object that would ordinarily require the strength of two men, possibly more. When they needed help with some heavy object that they themselves were trying to manage alone, William was always the first one they would call upon.

Competitions like the one he had just won were for awhile commonplace events in William's life. He took on all comers. And always won. Everywhere he went there was likely to be some boy or man, like Ike Johnson, waiting to challenge him to some feat of strength or endurance.

In the beginning, William enjoyed the challenges. However, winning so easily, sometimes without even exerting himself, he soon tired of the sport. He was also, in truth, more than a little sensitive to the resentment that he saw in the eyes of some of the men that he had humiliated so easily. Many did not see this as just a bit of sport, for some of them had openly boasted that they would be the one to beat Jackman.

William eventually tried to limit his participation in such games to garden parties and times where everyone, especially young boys, could participate with him and with each other in an atmosphere of fun and enjoyment. He developed small strategies to deflect the overtures of those wanting to pit themselves against his, by now, legendary prowess. He would turn back most would-be opponents with some joke or witty comment. When that didn't work, a cold, hard stare would usually do the trick.

Only twice did anyone persist beyond that point. In the first incident, the belligerent challenger, enraged at William's refusal to be baited and determined to engage him no matter what, had to be forcibly restrained by onlookers who thwarted the man's attempt to rush at William with obvious intent to do him harm. Somewhat shaken by the incident, although he never said much about it, William determined after this to be even more discreet and diplomatic in trying to fend off the endless challenges still put to him wherever he went.

In the second incident, the denied challenger rushed at William without warning as he walked away, striking him a glancing blow to his head and shoulders. Unhurt, but shocked and incensed, William felt a momentary surge of rage greater than he had ever felt before. Never in his lifetime had he been hit in anger by another man. His assailant, seeing the grim expression on William's face, immediately realized the folly of his actions and attempted to flee from the scene. But William, moving faster than anyone had ever seen him move before, seized the man before he could travel more than a few feet. Trying with great effort to control the rage that welled up inside him, which threatened to cloud his own judgement, William carried his now helpless opponent by the scruff of the neck and the seat of his pants to the outer edge of the wharf. Then, to the great delight of the crowd, he deposited the man, pleading and struggling, in ten feet of icy cold water.

Ironically, the embarrassed man who climbed out of the water a few seconds later would, in time, serve as a crew member under William's captaincy and become his good friend and a lifelong supporter.

Although he had previously accompanied his father on short fishing voyages a few times, William participated in the codfishery for the first time on a full-time basis in 1855. Unlike their counterparts in Conception Bay and the north-east coast of Newfoundland who pursued the Labrador fishery in larger schooners, the vast majority of Southern Shore fishermen operated inshore. They usually worked in one to four-man crews, close enough to shore to be able to return to the comfort and safety of their homes after each day of fishing. With one of the richest fishing grounds in the world right on their own doorstep, there was little need to venture much farther afield. The baited handlines and small nets that they employed yielded remarkable results from such primitive, labour-intensive methods. It would be another twenty years before the invention of the codtrap would revolutionize the fishing industry and make the plight of Newfoundland's fishermen a little more endurable. The markets of England and eastern Europe, in the meantime, could absorb every quintal of fish that the waters of Newfoundland could produce.

William's first year in the fishing industry was spent with the Powers, John and his father Nicholas, working inshore from a twenty-six-foot skiff not far from their home community of Renews. Having missed his opportunity to join the crew of the *Marian* the previous year because of his experience on the barrens and his injuries, he still had a strong desire to try his hand at fishing independently of his father and the family business. Although he would have liked to have had his son with him on the *Fanny Bloomer*, Thomas did not object too strenuously. In fact, he was secretly a bit pleased because with William still at home, he himself would not be as worried about Catherine and the rest of his family while he was away.

The area that William and the Powers fished stretched from Renews Head to Aquaforte, an expanse of water covering some twenty-odd square miles. Each morning before first light, he and John would do most of the rowing out to the fishing grounds, while the older man sat in the stern of the boat getting the handlines and bait organized for the day. Sometimes, if they had a fair wind, their skiff would be helped along by a little jib that was supported through a hole in the forward thawt. When they arrived at the fishing ground, they worked two handlines apiece, one on either side of the boat, hauling in the line hand-over-hand as quickly as possible whenever they felt a fish take the hook. Usually they fished until late afternoon or, on exceptionally slow days, into the early evening, pausing only to eat the meagre lunch that they had brought along with them. Sometimes they would cook a freshly caught fish in the sand-filled half barrel that Nicholas had placed near the boat's fore-cuddy.

The long row back home, although tiring after a full day of fishing, afforded William on most days the opportunity for a quick swim. Feeling cleansed and refreshed, his short dip always gave him renewed energy for the work of gutting, cleaning, and storing that had to be done before the three men could finally call their day's work complete.

On several occasions during his stint with the Powers, they found themselves scurrying for the shelter of some small cove or island when the wind or rain became too strong for them to safely fish from their small boat. Many long, miserable hours, which on a couple of occasions stretched into days and nights, were spent in this manner waiting for the weather to improve enough to enable them to make their way home again. At other times, they would be so beset by fog that William, not yet a seasoned seaman, often became completely disoriented. But Nicholas Power had an extraordinary nose for direction and brought them home safely every time.

The year that William spent with the Powers was a good learning experience and the beginning of a lifetime of work on the sea. It was not, however, a very productive year. At the end of the season, none of them had very much to show for their efforts. While others around them fished the same grounds with considerable success, Nicholas Power did not seem to have the ability of most of the other fishermen in the area, or the luck, to find the fish that concentrated in teeming masses in the deep, cold, plankton-rich waters of the Southern Shore. This, perhaps more than anything else, contributed to the state of poverty in which the Powers constantly found themselves.

The following year, at the age of fifteen, William finally joined his father on the *Fanny Bloomer*. As his father had hoped, William was by then an able and willing worker, more than capable of doing a man's full share of the work that had to be done. He got along with everyone on the schooner and was treated by all as just another crew member, not the captain's son. William would have wanted it no other way.

While the Jackman family's fishing business continued to grow and flourish, their original arrangement as buying agent for Bowring Brothers was still an important part of it. In the year that William turned seventeen, Thomas placed him in charge of this part of the business while he himself concentrated on other aspects of the family business operations in Renews and Spotted Island.

In contrast to some of the other mercantile interests in Newfoundland at that time, Bowring Brothers Limited was a relative newcomer, having only recently emerged as a major power in the Island's fishing and sealing industries. Founded some thirty-odd years earlier as a small store on Duckworth Street in St. John's, the firm had diversified very slowly through the acquisition of a couple of small schooners for the export trade with Great Britain and Europe. Remotely managed from Exeter, England, the company did not achieve the real growth and expansion that would eventually make it one of the wealthiest merchant firms in the history of Newfoundland until local control was assumed by Charles Tricks Bowring, the oldest son of its founder, Benjamin Bowring. Under Charles Tricks' guiding influence and aggressive leadership, the firm grew rapidly, increasing its fleet of fishing and sealing schooners many times over in the span of a few short years.

Despite his young age, William, like his father before him, readily earned the respect and trust of Bowring Brothers. They quickly came to recognize his intelligence, his maturity and his extraordinary ability to safely and efficiently guide their schooners and their crews. When they acquired the first of their steam powered ships a few years later, William would be their first and obvious choice to be her captain. They supported him in his efforts to qualify for his Master's Certificate, which he obtained before he reached his nineteenth birthday, one of the youngest Newfoundlanders ever to accomplish this feat.

Although he still occasionally sailed with his father on the *Fanny Bloomer*, much of William's time from the age of seventeen to his mid-twenties was spent running the Bowring's part of the business as captain of a progression of schooners that included the *Shipworth*, the *Sarah Ann*, and the *Margaret*. His favourite was the *Shipworth*. Ninety feet in length, this large schooner was ideally suited to the purpose of collecting salted fish from the settlements on the east and north-east coasts of Newfoundland for transfer to Bowring's premises in St. John's and eventual export to Europe. More stable, even in rough waters, than most other schooners, the trustworthy *Shipworth* brought William and his crew safely home from many voyages. Its only real brush with disaster, (until it was eventually driven ashore during a windstorm almost eleven years later, by which time it was owned by another firm) was a minor collision with another fog-bound fishing schooner off Torbay on the St. John's Shore. But William had been able to spot the other vessel in time to avert serious impact, and the two schooners safely passed with only a gentle scraping against each other's sides. Such incidents were commonplace in the fishing industry at that time, and were generally accepted as occupational hazards by the men who manned these vessels.

Trips to Trinity, Bonavista, Twillingate, and the many other settlements along the north-east coast were a new and exciting experience for William. Time spent in some of these communities would often be only a few hours, but at other times their stay might be for a number of days. He and the crew always looked forward to these stops as a well-deserved break, for on the schooner itself there was very little time for relaxing. He enjoyed meeting the people of these fishing communities, and established many lifetime friendships and associations.

One day in late September in 1857, while the *Shipworth* was taking on fish in Trinity, William and the crew finished their work for the day a little earlier than expected. Taking advantage of the rare opportunity to do some exploring, William wandered around the town, lost in the bustle and the smells and sounds all around him. Although he had been in Trinity before, he had never taken the time to really get to know the community. He was greatly impressed by what he now saw. He could see why Trinity was generally recognized as the fishing capital of Newfoundland and why every year hundreds of fishing and sealing vessels made Trinity their departure point. Here they provisioned and prepared for the long trip to Labrador or to the ice-fields of northern Newfoundland.

William observed that the bustling community had two large and busy shipyards, a courthouse, even a jail. He also noted that the style and quality of most of the houses were superior to those that he had seen in most other places. A roughly worded sign on one of the larger buildings informed him that Trinity had claimed for itself a small niche in world medical history fifty-seven years earlier when one of its residents, a Dr. John Clinch, administered the first smallpox vaccination ever given in the New World. William also thought that St. Paul's Church, located in the centre of the community, was one of the largest and most impressive that he had ever seen, despite the fact that it was Anglican and dwarfed the tiny Roman Catholic Church just a few hundred yards away.

A quick tally told William that the sheltered harbour that Richard Whitbourne (later Sir Richard) had once called "the best and largest harbour in all the land," held no less than fifty schooners on that day. Their crews swelled the roads and pathways of the community to overflowing. He was so absorbed in his own thoughts that he didn't notice the girl walking towards him until he bumped into her. Embarrassed, he retrieved her hat that had fallen to the ground and apologized profusely for his clumsiness. As he was about to turn away, he realized that the girl looked vaguely familiar to him. Never too shy to speak his mind, William said, "You know, I'm sure I seen you somewhere before."

Before he could say anything further, the young woman replied, "I know you, too. You're William Jackman, aren't you? You and your father were in our house in Trepassey one time, a few years ago."

"Yes, I know now. You're Mr. Burbridge's daughter."

"That's right, I'm Bridget Burbridge. I'm here with my father for a few days. Then we're going to St. John's. We're moving back to live there again. He's going back to work in J & W Boyd's store again."

As they talked, the young man and woman found themselves wandering out to a point of land known by everybody in the community as Hog's Nose, where they spent the best part of an hour looking at the sights of the harbour and the lighthouse directly across from them on Fort Point. Beyond the lighthouse could be seen the vast, unbroken expanse of ocean that stretched eastward for two thousand miles, all the way to Europe. Used to the constant smell of fish and brine, their nostrils were not overly offended by the stench of pothead whales being rendered into oil on one of the beaches on the other side of the Trinity Harbour's south-west arm. This activity that they witnessed was the forerunner of a major whaling operation that would be started on that same site years later by a Norwegian firm, headed by a man named Nils Neilssen.

It was almost dark when William walked Bridget back to the schooner on which she was staying. It was the beginning of a courtship that would see them become man and wife in Renews three years later.

William was eighteen when he made his first trip to the coast of Labrador with his father in the *Fanny Bloomer*. He immediately fell in love with this wild and magnificent land in the North. As the *Fanny Bloomer* wended her way down the coast towards her northernmost destination of Hopedale, William was enchanted with the rugged coastline and its many tiny villages and hamlets. Brief stops were made in Battle Harbour, Port Hope Simpson, and Cartwright, where they stayed a day or two in each settlement. William was particularly impressed with the great tableland that swept westward all the way from the very edge of Groswater Bay to a far distant snowcapped mountain many miles inland. He had never seen anything like it before. Two days later, their sojourn into the 150-mile indraft of Hamilton Inlet brought them within the grandeur of the Mealy Mountains, one of the most majestic mountain ranges east of the Rocky Mountains in Canada's far west. Accustomed to the flatness of the sea and the low hills and barrens of Newfoundland's Southern Shore, the Mealy Mountains were one of the greatest spectacles that William had ever witnessed.

At they progressed further northward, William noted the increasing number of aboriginal people in the coastal villages that they visited. These natives were known as Naskapi in the southernmost areas of Labrador and as Montagnais further north. Both groups were nomadic hunters and referred to themselves collectively as Innu and had only partially integrated with their white neighbours. Although they took advantage of the guns and other tools that had been introduced by settlers from Newfoundland

and Europe years earlier, they still preferred to live by themselves in small bands to hunt and fish in their own traditional ways.

William took a great interest in the Innu. On his numerous future voyages to Labrador, he would meet many of these aboriginal people firsthand and would try to learn as much as he could about their culture and history. Over time, most of the Innu along the Labrador coast would come to count William as a friend and as a man that they could trust. He especially endeared himself to them when he once took one of their seriously injured leaders on his schooner and transported the man to Cartwright where he received the medical attention that saved his life.

Many captains would turn the Innu away when they tried to board their vessels, but William never did. They were always welcomed and sometimes sat for hours in the forecastle of the vessel, drinking cup after cup of hot tea and depleting the vessel's supply of ship's biscuits. Before biting into the hard tack that was usually given to them, they would always first ask if there were any soda crackers, their favourite. They liked to soak them in their tea. William took care, however, never to give the Innu the hard liquor that they sometimes managed to get from some of the other ships. He knew that they were unaccustomed to consuming rum and other strong spirits and that they sometimes did violent and unpredictable things when they did so. Occasionally some unscrupulous captain or settler would ply these usually placid aboriginal people with rum just to see what would happen, sometimes with sad or tragic results.

To William, the Innu seemed very different from the few Inuit that he also saw from time to time in some of the more northern villages that they visited. These nomads of the north, together with the Innu, were usually referred to by early white settlers as Eskimos. Most white people made no distinction between the two groups and sometimes also referred to them collectively as Esquimau, Esquimaux-Indians or Huskimaw. Some simply called them the Savages or Savage-Indians. The two groups, however, had little association with each other, usually keeping to their own territories and maintaining their own lifestyles and cultures.

The traditional Labrador Inuit were the most easterly of several distinct but culturally related aboriginal groups that occupied the vast frozen tundra of the northern Arctic. Living along the coast of Labrador between Hopedale in the south and Cape Chidley in the far north, they referred to themselves as Suhinimiut, people of the sun, or simply as "The People." Ever protective of their own land areas and customs, they were somewhat leery of the Innu, the Skraelings[8] that eventually drove the Norse Vikings from their foothold in L'Anse aux Meadows[9], and usually kept their distance. The Innu did likewise and seldom strayed north of their more southerly domain.

William noted that the Inuit were also much more guarded and reserved in their attitudes toward the white settlers along the Labrador coast than were the Innu. In all his years in Labrador, he was never able to form the same kind of close relationship with any of these shy and private people, as he had with the Innu.

Reluctant to ever go below deck until the need for sleep finally forced him to do so, he would never forget the sights and sounds of Labrador and the peace and solitude that he felt as the *Fanny Bloomer* plodded on toward her destination. He would always remember these moments as some of the most peaceful and happiest of his life.

In the clear, star-filled nights of the north, the *Fanny Bloomer* continued to sail quietly northward. The sea ahead and the coastline on the port side of the vessel were clearly visible for many miles. The men of the schooner's eight-man crew each took a four-hour shift at the wheel while the others slept below or did other jobs. It was during his shift, at four o'clock one beautifully clear morning just before daybreak off Indian Harbour, that William had what he later said was the only supernatural encounter of his life. Alone at the wheel, he was lost as usual in his thoughts. The aurora borealis lent a surreal effect to his surroundings. The schooner slipped slowly and silently through the calm water. His reverie was suddenly interrupted by the sensation that he wasn't alone. He would swear to his dying day that when he turned his head, he saw for a fleeting moment or two the ethereal wraithlike figure of Aunt Maggie standing at the railing. He blinked his eyes several times to assure himself that he wasn't dreaming. And then she was gone. Strangely, he was not unnerved by the incident. If anything, he was oddly comforted by it. A love that could transcend time and space could do him no harm. Aunt Maggie had come to say goodbye.

When Thomas replaced him at the wheel two hours later, William told him, "Father, I think Aunt Maggie died last night." Thomas stared hard at his son for a long time. Neither man spoke any further. William went below deck for his breakfast, and the *Fanny Bloomer* journeyed on.

On their homeward journey, its hold almost filled to capacity with the fish that they had collected, the *Fanny Bloomer* stopped in at Spotted Island Harbour, a small island community located just north of Black Tickle near the entrance to Groswater Bay, where part of the Jackman family business was located. Surrounded by some of the most prolific fishing grounds in Labrador, the tiny settlement's small population of *livyeres*[10] was greatly increased in the summer months by the large number of migratory fishing vessels that ventured north from the bays of Newfoundland.

There, William and his father stayed overnight at the home of Samuel Holwell, a long-time friend of Thomas, while the rest of the *Fanny Bloomer's* crew remained onboard the vessel. Samuel's brother, John, joined them, and the men talked long into the night. When Thomas finally retired for the night, William stayed a little longer, intrigued by the tales that the Holwell's told him about their life on a small island off the Labrador coast. Little did the three men sitting around the kitchen table on that pleasant night know that a strange twist of fate would throw them together again eight years later on the northern shore of Spotted Island for one of the most amazing rescue operations ever known in Labrador's long and turbulent maritime history.

Late in November, William and Thomas finally returned home to Renews at the completion of a very successful season. It was one of the best they ever recorded. One of Catherine's first comments when she saw her husband and oldest son again for the first time in many months was, "Oh, William, oh my oh my, where's my little b'y gone? Sure, you're grown bigger than your father." Indeed, the six months of hard work at sea had fleshed out William's frame, and he stood nearly an inch taller than he had when he left home the previous June.

As they ate the supper that Catherine prepared for them, the two men tried to catch up on the things that had happened in the community while they were away. Both men were saddened, but not surprised, when Catherine quietly told them that Aunt Maggie had passed away. The frail, generous woman who had given so much to the community that she loved, had passed away peacefully in her sleep at the age of eighty-six. Neither Thomas nor William felt the need to ask when she had died.

As the years passed, William often thought about Aunt Maggie and the pleasant moments he had spent in her company. Once, when asked about the occurrence on the schooner that morning in Black Tickle, he laughed jokingly and said, "You know, the Southern Shore got more spirits and tokens than it got people. Sure everyone sees them all the time, except me. They're all so ugly and fearsome that people are frightened to death to go out after dark. But me, the only ghost I ever seen was poor old Aunt Maggie, and she looked even sweeter then than she did when she was alive."

Typical Labrador sailing schooners. Circa 1900.

"Wooden Wall" steamers made their first appearance on the ice fields of northern Newfoundland in 1863. Circa 1900.

Sealing

OH IN THE SPRING THE FLIPPERS BRING
TO LAWYERS, CLERKS OR BEAGLE;
WE FOUGHT BRAVE NEPTUNE UP AND DOWN
AND CARRIED HOME THE EAGLE.

— "Sealers' Song"
Author unknown

*W*hile the cod fishery was William's main interest, he was also a sealer. In his lifetime, he went "to the ice" no less than twelve times. At the age of sixteen, like hundreds of other men from the bays and coves of eastern Newfoundland, he threw his duffle bag over his back and made his way to St. John's where many of the island's sealing schooners were being prepared for the annual seal hunt. Unlike some who went to the city with only the slightest prospect of getting a berth, William was assured of a spot on his father's ship, the *Fanny Bloomer*, despite his age and the fact that he had no previous sealing experience.

Pursued initially by the fishermen of Notre Dame Bay and White Bay as a means of supplementing the predominantly fish-laden diet of their families, the seal fishery in the mid-1800's was still a fledgling part of Newfoundland's island economy. Stimulated by the increasing demand for oil to keep the lamps of England and other European countries burning, the annual seal hunt gradually spread northward to the "Front," the vast expanse of sea to the east and north-east of Newfoundland. There, the immense ice-fields carried south each spring by the Labrador Current, brought with them the great seal herds of the far north, including thousands of whitecoats whelped only a few weeks earlier. The hunt, which would eventually expand to the Gulf of St. Lawrence, provided an additional source of income for many Newfoundland fishermen.

Adult harp seals weighing several hundred pounds and the even larger hood seals produced the greatest yields when their fat-layered carcasses were rendered into oil. These fierce creatures were, however, much harder to kill than the smaller whitecoats. Their aggressiveness and inclination to attack when confronted posed considerable danger to the men who pursued them armed only with gaffs and clubs. Consequently, the final harvest of most vessels usually contained a high percentage of the younger mammals. In later years, when the advent of household electricity eliminated the need for such great quantities of lamp oil, the emphasis of the hunt would change and focus almost entirely on the soft, luxurious pelts of the newborn whitecoats to meet the new fashion styles of Europe and North America.

The short sealing season, which usually lasted from early March to late April, also spawned a number of other important spin-off industries. Coopers were in great demand to construct the huge vats and barrels that were needed to transport the seal oil across the ocean, and tanneries were needed to cure the lesser-valued seal pelts into the rough leather that was also destined for the markets of Europe. Some of the more powerful merchants exploiting the cod fishery at that time maintained their own large ocean-going sailing vessels to ship salted fish to their European markets each summer and fall. They could now employ these same vessels in the spring for the additional purpose of transporting seal oil and leather, thus greatly increasing their value and the return on their investment.

The life of the sealers, or "swilers" as they were called in some areas, was not an easy one. The schooners they boarded for the seal fishery were the same ones that, a few months earlier, were employed in the cod fishery. The normal six to ten-man fishing crews were now expanded to thirty or forty men or as many as the vessel could practically hold to maximize the number of seals taken. Temporary benches were constructed below deck where the men slept in extremely cramped quarters, especially in the latter part of the voyage when this space began to be encroached upon by the growing number of seal carcasses. Divided into watches, usually four or five to a ship, the men spent all day, from first light until dark, on the ice searching for seals. Their day's catch was usually stored on ice pans to be collected later by their vessel. But sometimes ice conditions and other factors forced the men to haul the day's yield of carcasses back to the vessel themselves.

Their subsistence diet on the ice consisted mainly of hard bread and salted pork. Water to quench their thirst was obtained from small indentations in the ice or from some nearby ice pinnacle. Some men, ravenous from their exertions, occasionally ate the raw hearts and livers of the seals that they caught. Their main meal for the day, upon returning to their ships, was usually salted pork and figgy duffs[11], sometimes accompanied by a dollop of molasses and as many cups of scalding tea as they could consume. When their hunger still wasn't totally satisfied, they sometimes cooked a seal carcass or a few flippers on the ice or in a barrel on the deck of the schooner.

Sealing was not only an occupation of hardship and deprivation, but one of the most perilous and hazardous occupations of the world at that time. It remains so today, despite modern technology and the vastly superior vessels and support structures now employed. The sail-powered schooners used before the advent of steam-powered ships, although agile and speedy in open waters, were no match for the harsh conditions of the ice-fields into which they ventured. Trying to follow open leads of water, these vessels and their crews often found themselves trapped in heavy ice, unable to move in any direction. Every sealer, at some point in his sealing years, experienced many long anxious hours, sometimes days at a time, locked in shifting, buckling ice that grated relentlessly against the fragile sides of his vessel. Many trapped sealing schooners, with no means of propulsion other than their now useless sails, were crushed and destroyed by the enormous pressure of the ice. Their crews, if they were lucky, swarmed onto ice pans and waited to be rescued by some other vessel in the area. Often they were not and perished in great numbers where they stood.

Yet, despite the massive loss of men and ships, the seal fishery expanded and grew to become a vital part of Newfoundland's economy. In 1863, the first steam-powered vessels owned by Baine Johnston & Co. and Walter Grieve & Co. made their appearance on the ice-fields. Three years later, in 1866, Bowring Brothers followed the lead of their competitors when they acquired their first steamer, the *Hawke*. With their strongly reinforced hulls and own source of power, these newer vessels, which were often referred to as "wooden walls," were not nearly as vulnerable to the dangers of the pack ice as were the traditional sailing schooners. Much larger than the schooners, they could also accommodate crews that often numbered two hundred or more.

William's initial venture to the ice at the age of sixteen in the *Fanny Bloomer* was a startling revelation to him. Accustomed to the relative cleanliness and neatness of the fishing schooners that he had served on, he was not prepared for the filthy conditions and squalor that confronted him on the sealing vessels. Men slept and ate in the midst of thousands of bloody seal carcasses. Their clothing and bodies, even their food, could not escape the grime and gore that surrounded them. Sometimes, as the number of seals harvested began to overflow into the areas occupied by the temporary sleeping benches, men often found themselves actually sleeping on top of the great pile of carcasses. Many, William included, preferred to sleep and eat on deck whenever they could, even in cold and freezing weather. The stench of blubber, blood, and men unwashed in weeks was more than they could stand.

Even as late as the 1950's the lot of the sealers had improved only marginally. Although the sealing vessels by then were much larger and equipped with electronic communications and spotter planes to help them find the "main patch," and provided the men with better food and sleeping accommodations, the actual work on the ice was still just as hard as a hundred years previously and the dangers still as imminent. And, after three to six weeks at the Front or the Gulf, many sealers still returned home just as dirty and unshaven, and as lice-ridden as their forebears. One woman who was returning home from Water Street on the city bus in the early 1950's moved to the rear and covered her face when her brother, whom she loved dearly, boarded the bus. He had just gotten off his sealing vessel, and she did not wish to be seen with him in his filthy state. Despite her efforts to avoid him, he spotted her anyway and to her utter mortification, he hugged her in front of all the other passengers and planted a great mushy kiss on her cheek.

Apart from the normal hardships and deprivations of life on a sealing schooner, and a couple of dunkings in the frigid water when he miscalculated the distance when copying from one ice pan to another, William's first trip to the ice was relatively uneventful. Even though the voyage had been reasonably successful, William was disappointed in his small share of the proceeds from the voyage.

Yet by January of the following year, William found himself looking forward to his second trip to the ice. Hardened and seasoned somewhat by the experience of the previous year, he now knew what to expect.

Only a week into the hunt, the *Fanny Bloomer* was well ahead of its pace of the previous year. Having found a large patch early, the men had nearly fifteen hundred seals onboard, with another seven or eight hundred carcasses on the ice waiting to be picked up.

After one particularly hard day, William was informed by his father that he was being reassigned to another watch for the next few days. One of the men from the group to which he was being loaned had severely injured himself with his long flensing knife while skinning a seal, and another sealer was too sick in his bunk to perform his usual duties. William, although disappointed because he liked the men and the comradery of his own watch, offered no resistance. Like always, he did as he was ordered, determined to do his best no matter what came his way.

At 5:00 a.m. William, with sealing gaff and hauling rope, scrambled over the side with the other eleven men of his new watch. Making their way in a southeasterly direction across the rafted ice, the men marched almost three miles before they saw the first sign of seals. It was a small patch, and by noon they had only a dozen or so carcasses on the ice. Marking their catch with one of the flags that they had brought along for that purpose, they decided to venture a little further eastward, where Luke Jordan, the master of the watch, was certain that he had seen another patch some distance away.

When they reached the area, they were rewarded for their efforts. A much larger herd of harp seals and their whitecoat off-spring lounged lazily on the ice floes ahead. A few of the older and larger harp seals, mostly mothers very protective of their young, growled and shook their heads menacingly at the men as they approached. For the most part, however, the herd ignored the men that had come to kill them.

Totally occupied with the slaughter of the seals, the men failed to notice the change in the direction of the wind, which now blew briskly from the north-west, and it wasn't until they felt the first snowflakes on their faces that they realized that the fine weather of the morning was degenerating rapidly.

Jordan, having experienced sudden storms on the ice before, told his men, "We better be getting back, b'ys. I think there's a bit of weather comin' on."

Flagging their catch, the men of the watch headed back in the direction of their vessel. As often happens in the northern reaches of the Atlantic Ocean, storms and blizzards arise and intensify so quickly that men are caught off guard before they have time to react and reach shelter. Only minutes into their long walk home, the men found themselves being battered by freezing winds and driving snow that froze instantly to their clothing and faces, blinding them as they plodded onward. A few of the men grumbled from time to time and urged Jordan to let them stop for a few minutes to catch their breath. But the watchmaster, realizing the urgency of their situation, kept them going, prodding them along whenever they lagged or faltered.

After walking a little more than a mile in the direction of the schooner that they could no longer see, William and the other men were alarmed and dismayed when they discovered that the expanse of ice on which they were travelling had separated from the ice-field ahead. An open lead of water measuring some fifty feet across now stood between them and the safety and warmth of their vessel. A further check in all directions verified the fact that they were now stranded on a large island of ice that was being driven by the wind and the tide eastward, away from the *Fanny Bloomer* and the other vessels in the area.

The sealers realized now for the first time that they were in extreme danger. William and the other men prepared to spend the night on the open ice, hoping that Thomas Jackman and the *Fanny Bloomer* would somehow be able to find them in the storm. Using chunks of ice and snow, they erected a semi-circular wall to shelter themselves as best they could from the wind and driving snow. They remembered that they had passed a small cluster of seals a short distance back. A few of the men, thinking that the seals might come in handy later as food or shelter, retraced their steps to kill the five small whitecoats that still lay on the ice blissfully oblivious to the raging weather. The seals were dragged back to the small enclosure, quickly skinned, and their carcasses added to the barricade of ice and snow. The pelts, although bloody and oily, might help to protect the feet and hands of the men in the freezing temperature.

There the stranded sealers waited. They talked and sometimes sang to keep themselves awake and alert. As the hours passed and darkness set in, the temperature plummeted to almost twenty degrees below zero. Some of the men, bitterly cold, hungry, and frightened, grew morose and disheartened.

"We'll never get in out of this, b'ys," one man moaned, "we're all done for, I knows it."

"Yes, b'y, by the time they finds us, sure we'll all be froze to death."

William shared the concerns of the other men. The details of his boyhood ordeal on the barrens of Renews ran vividly through his mind. He could almost again feel the trembling of Annie's tiny body against his and his feeling of despair and disbelief when she died. The sadness that gripped him brought him to the realization that his own life, after all he had lived through before, might now end here, with him frozen to death on a drifting ice-pan in the desolate ice-fields of northern Newfoundland. He found himself drifting off in a stupor induced by his sense of foreboding, the great sorrow that he felt, and the storm raging around him. He struggled to rouse himself from his lethargy. Somewhere he found the resolve to tell himself, "No, by God. It won't happen again. I won't let it. We're all going to survive this. I don't care, I'm not going to die out here on the ice. And nobody else is either."

Somehow finding new strength and determination, he forced himself to stand up. Once on his feet, he then berated the other men, shouting, "Come on, b'ys, get up. You got to try to save yourselves. You all got wives and children, and here you are, giving up without even trying. Sure they'd all be ashamed of you if they knew what you were acting like now. Come on now, you can do it if you try. Just think about your families."

He continued his unrelenting harangue until he finally bullied and coaxed the other men to their feet too. He then forced them to walk around in a large circle, each man holding tightly to the man in front of him, trying to keep themselves awake and the blood flowing in their veins. When someone started a well-known sea chant, the other men gradually joined in. Jordan, with William's assistance, managed to set fire to one of the whitecoat carcasses that they had retrieved earlier. The high flames and heat produced by the layers of oily fat gave some warmth and comfort to the freezing men. The first carcass burned for almost half an hour before it finally sputtered out in the wind. The men waited another forty minutes before they attempted to light the next one. They realized that the remaining four carcasses might have to last them a long time if they were to survive the night.

The fourth carcass was burning brightly when the men were startled by the sudden clanging of a ship's bell that came out of the darkness of the night, seemingly right upon them. Thomas Jackman, following a lead of water that miraculously stretched in the direction he knew the watch had taken, had come to search for his son and his men. Spotting the sealers' fire through the blinding snow, he was able to rescue them from further danger and bring them safely onboard the *Fanny Bloomer*.

In the eleven years that he spent "going to the ice," this was the closest William ever came to real disaster. On a few other occasions, he and his companions found themselves stranded away from their vessel for short periods of time during storms or when they were lost in the snow or fog, but they always managed to somehow get back to their vessel in time. He never again faced the same peril that he had that night on the drifting ice-pan.

In a similar set of circumstances, fifty-eight years later, the crew of the *Newfoundland*, captained by Wesley Kean, the son of Newfoundland's most famous sealing master, Abraham Kean, spent fifty-three hours stranded on the ice in a blinding blizzard. Before they were found, seventy-eight men had died of drowning or exposure. Sadly, it was revealed afterwards that the wireless that could have saved them had been removed from the *Newfoundland* only weeks earlier as a means of reducing the overhead costs of the ship's owners.

William made his third trip to the ice in 1855, this time as the eighteen-year-old captain of the *Shipworth*, having obtained his master's certificate just a few months earlier. Many were skeptical of the ability of such a young, unproven master to make a successful voyage. The bumper load of seals that he brought home five weeks later, however, dispelled all doubts.

He continued to make annual sealing voyages as the captain of various schooners until he became captain of the *Hawke* in 1862. As the master of the much larger, steam-powered vessel, he found everything to be very different from the sailing schooners that he had always worked on and sometimes captained. However, he quickly learned the ways of the ship that he would come to love and which would become an important part of his life. He was a demanding taskmaster who accepted nothing less than a full, honest effort from the men he directed. He could also be a hard-nosed disciplinarian when he had to be. But he was fair, ensuring that the workload of the ship was distributed equally amongst the crew. His crews respected him and more importantly, trusted his judgement and ability to take them out to sea and bring them back home safely, time and time again.

A few years later the great respect that Bowring Brothers had for Jackman as a sealing captain was evident when they honoured him by having their newest steamer, the *Eagle*, especially constructed for him in Dundee, Scotland.

William remained captain of the *Eagle* until his death in 1877. In his twenty-two years as a fishing and sealing captain, he gained a reputation as a master who put the safety of his vessels and their crews above all else. His unblemished record still stands as a model for captains and ships everywhere.

Captain William Jackman and Captain Arthur Jackman.

The Rescue
At Spotted Island

WHEN I REACH THAT LAST BIG SHOAL
WHERE THE GROUND SWELLS BREAK ASUNDER,
WHERE THE WILD SANDS ROLL TO THE SURGE'S TOLL,
LET ME BE A MAN AND TAKE IT
WHEN MY DORY FAILS TO MAKE IT.

— "Let Me Fish Off Cape St. Mary's"
Otto P. Kelland

*S*potted Island, so called for the large white patches that mark its shoreline, is a mass of bare rock and stunted, windswept spruce lying a few miles off the coast of eastern Labrador near the entrance to Groswater Bay. Millions of years earlier this once subterranean mountain, like the hundreds of other islands that dot Newfoundland's north-east coastline and the coast of Labrador, had ruptured the ocean floor. It then pushed its way upward, propelled by the cataclysmic volcanic pressures that eventually shaped the land masses of Newfoundland and Labrador, finally coming to rest a few miles south-east of the long indraft of water known today as Hamilton Inlet.

The populated south-east corner of Spotted Island had long been a safe haven for ships seeking shelter from the fierce storms that ravage the Labrador coast each year. The north side of the island, by contrast, except for one small semi-sheltered indentation known as Griffin's Harbour, is almost totally exposed to the cold, piercing winds that sweep down relentlessly from the vast ice-fields of the frozen Arctic.

The waters surrounding Spotted Island were once one of the richest fishing grounds in the world, especially the area immediately south-east of the island known as Domino Run. Every year from the 1700's onward, the island's permanent population of forty livyeres temporarily tripled in May or early June by the arrival of dozens of sturdy two-masted schooners and their crews that sailed north from Conception Bay, Bonavista Bay, Trinity Bay, and other parts of the island to fish in these fertile northern waters. These migratory fishermen, often called Stationers[12], usually set up their summer fishing stations on the north side of the Island in Griffin Harbour or on the nearby Island of Ponds. There the men and women cured and stored the cod that were caught by the schooners' crews using handlines, trawls, seines, and other small nets. Year after year, almost without fail, these same fish-laden schooners made their way home in October or November, the season of sudden gales, hugging the coastline all the way back to avoid being overtaken by a sudden storm.

At 5:00 a.m. on October 9, 1867, John Holwell sat at his kitchen table, watching the faint light of dawn filter through the east window that overlooked most of Spotted Island Harbour. He was trying to decide whether he would venture out in the choppy water in his 22-foot skiff or wait until the seas subsided a little. His wife, Madeline, had arisen a half-hour earlier to fire up the old cast-iron stove to kill the chill of the cold morning air and to prepare her husband's breakfast. As she moved about the kitchen, she thought ahead to the workday that would see her do the usual neverending household chores—feed her children, turn the fish on the flake a couple of times, tend the few vegetables in the garden that had not yet been harvested, and see to her few hens and sheep. John would expect a good hardy supper to be waiting for him when he came home from his work. Some days, like today, when he was not out on the water, he might also drop home for a quick mug up at midday.

John reflected that it had been a good summer for him and his brother, Samuel. Their stage was filled almost to its full capacity with their seasons' catch. While they could have chosen any of several other vessels that plied these waters, he and Samuel had committed their catch to the *Hawke* and her captain, William Jackman. Through long association with him, they both knew that Jackman would do his utmost to ensure that they were paid a fair price, and that not too many of their fish would be culled out as the lower grade usually set aside for the poorer markets of the West Indies.

Unbeknownst to Holwell, the *Hawke* was at that very moment steaming northward just fifty miles south of Spotted Island. As William Jackman paced the deck in the morning's early light, he felt the same apprehension that clearly showed on the faces of all the other men. Even though the sky was reasonably clear and the sea was not rough enough to seriously hinder the *Hawke's* progress, her crew, to a man, sensed that something was not quite right.

Only minutes earlier, the reclusive Isaac Barnes, who sometimes went days without speaking, had approached William with his admonishment that, "Skipper, mark my words. We'll know it before this day is out. You wait and see." Having said his piece, the old man stalked away without further elaboration. William, strangely, shared the man's obvious anxiety. An hour and a half later, Barnes was back again to point out the pale bluish rings that circled the almost colourless sun like halos. William had seen these "sun hounds" only twice before in his lifetime. On both occasions they had heralded the onslaught of the most terrible, devastating storms that he had ever witnessed.

William's initial intention had been to continue to steam northward all the way to Hopedale and to stop in at Spotted Island and several other coastal communities later on their way back south. This morning, however, his instinct and intuition, honed by many years on the salt water, made him change his mind. He decided to make for Spotted Island Harbour instead, where, if necessary, they would wait out the storm that he now knew for certain was coming.

By the time the *Hawke* lay safely at anchor, the storm that would be one of the worst ever recorded on the Labrador coast,

was already in progress. Even though the sheltered harbour afforded excellent protection, William took the extra precaution of
double anchoring the *Hawke* fore and aft to ensure that the vessel
did not have too much leeway to swing about in the wind. Most of
the men went ashore to visit acquaintances that they had made
on their many previous trips to Spotted Island or to simply walk
about the small community to pass the rare idle time that they
now had on their hands. A few stayed on the ship.

William headed for the house of John Holwell, hoping that his
good friend would be at home or close by. Madeline, with the
spontaneous hospitality of all northern women, greeted him exu-
berantly, exclaiming, "William Jackman, why you're a sight for
sore eyes! I think you looks better every time I sees ya. Come in,
come in, b'y, and have a drop of tea. I expects you're looking for
John. He went down around the stage about an hour ago."

William hugged her, aware for the first time of the tiny boy
peering at him shyly from the safety of the folds of his mother's
billowing skirt. "Now that can't be little Alfie, can it? Sure he's
growing like a weed. Before you know it he'll be up and gone."
Reaching into his pocket, he pulled out the small sack of candy
that he always brought along as a treat for the Holwell children
and extended the bag to the little boy who, after first looking to
his mother for approval, gingerly reached in and took one.

William found John Holwell in the stage, working along with
Samuel trying to clear enough space in the crowded outbuilding
to accommodate the last of their summer's catch. The three men
chatted comfortably for almost an hour, mostly about the fishing
season now nearing its end and the weather that was intensifying
by the minute as they spoke.

"Now you'll be staying the night with us, won't you? Madeline
and the children will be some disappointed if you goes back to
your steamer. Sure, we still got a few turrs down in the well, and
we'll have a little scoff for ourselves. And a good game of cards."

Shortly after noon Holwell's oldest daughter, Rachel, came to
tell the men that their tea was on the table. "Mom says fer you to
come too, Uncle Samuel. We got plenty."

The three men continued their conversation as they ate. The two large bowls of pea soup that William drank were a pleasant diversion from the salt pork and potatoes that accompanied most of the meals served on the *Hawke*. As he wolfed down another slab of buttered bread and his second cup of tea, much hungrier than he had realized, William told the Holwells, "I think I'll go for a little walk. I've been on that steamer so long I don't think my legs are much good for walking anymore."

"I'll come with you, and you can tell me all the news from St. John's," replied John. "You coming, Samuel?"

"No, b'y, I don't think so. I still got a few things I wants to get done before dark. But you two go on without me."

Despite the severity of the weather, the two men walked through the tiny settlement for several minutes before they picked up one of the winding footpaths that led to the north side of the island. Hunched forward, chilled by the howling northeasterly wind, William pulled his collar up around his throat and thrust his hands deep into his pockets. At times the force of the wind stopped the men in their tracks. It was not much of a day for a stroll. The few partridgeberries that they saw as they walked along reminded William of his ordeal on the barrens of Renews many years earlier.

"William, b'y, perhaps we should go on back now. I pities any poor souls out on the water in this weather. You wouldn't catch me out there today for love nor money."

"In a few minutes, John. I just want to take a look over them cliffs to see how bad it is out there, and then we'll go back." William would later swear that something had compelled him to go on, urging him onward until they reached the open water.

Suddenly he stiffened. "John, did you hear that? That sounded like a gunshot."

"Go 'way, b'y, sure who'd be shooting out here in weather like this? That was just the wind or a bit of thunder."

"I don't know. But listen. I think I heard it again. Come on, let's have a look."

Increasing their pace in the face of the wind that ripped at their clothing and chilled their bodies, the two men quickly reached the crest of the cliffs that overlooked the vast expanse of ocean to the north. It was several seconds before a lull in the snow squall permitted them to see out over the water.

"Holy Mother of God!" The two men stood at the edge of the cliff, oblivious to the salty spray that stung their faces, stunned, as they tried to comprehend the spectacle before them.

Recovering from his initial shock, William's quick assessment told him that the schooner that he judged to be about five hundred feet from shore (later he would learn that the distance was actually closer to six hundred feet) was obviously disembowelled on a reef and was being pounded mercilessly by the massive waves that threatened to break her apart at any moment. In the driving snow, it was a few more seconds before he could make out the large number of people he saw clinging to the railing of the sharply tilted vessel. Fishing schooners of that size normally carried crews of a dozen or less, sometimes only four or five, and the figures he now saw on the stranded vessel far exceeded that number. He thought there must be close to twenty of them. He couldn't be certain, but from a distance, some of them appeared to be women.

Holwell was the first to find his voice. "William, what can we do? I can't see any way that they can get off from there by themselves, or any way we can get out to them."

"No, there's no way we could get a boat off in this water, even if we had one. She'd break up on the rocks or capsize before she could get any more than a few feet off. I can't see any way to get a line out there either."

As they both watched helplessly, the idea that would manifest itself into action a few minutes later was already forming in William's mind. "Tell you what," he told Holwell, "you go back and get some men and I'll stay here and keep watch. Bring back as much rope as you can carry. Go as fast as you can. I don't think that schooner can last much longer. I'd say another hour or two at the most."

As Holwell headed back toward Spotted Island Harbour for help, William scrambled down the steep embankment to the small rocky beach directly below. He thought he heard the cries of the stranded victims in the howling wind. When he looked out toward the schooner again, he saw that several of them were waving their arms, having obviously spotted him on the shore.

Disaster and sudden death were no strangers to William. During his lifetime many of his acquaintances, including several relatives and close friends, had lost their lives at sea or on the icefields of northern Newfoundland in some of the terrible tragedies that punctuate Newfoundland's turbulent and often tragic maritime history. Yet his heart ached for the poor people now facing certain death on the doomed schooner, only a couple of hundred yards from the safety of the shore. Their pitiful cries for help touched him deeply.

Almost without thinking, he found himself stripping off his clothing. Shedding his rubber boots, coat, and heavy flannel shirt, he was quickly down to his socks and underwear. He didn't yet know exactly what he would do. He only knew that he couldn't just stand by and watch these people perish without trying to do something to help them.

His first step into the water took away his breath. Never before had he known anything even remotely close to the paralyzing iciness that he now experienced. He felt excruciating pain all over his body. He was surprised by the fact that his shins seemed to be the worst of all. As he made his first few strokes, he remembered hearing somewhere that a man could only survive for a few minutes in the frigid waters of the North Atlantic. He knew that if he were to have any chance at all, he would have to keep moving.

He had great difficulty making headway against the huge waves and strong tides that pushed him back no matter how hard he tried to thrust his body forward. He discovered that by swimming underwater, surfacing on every sixth or seventh stroke to take air, he was able to make better progress. At times he thought that his lungs would burst. With great determination, he battled on. The three or four minutes that had elapsed since he had first entered the water seemed liked an eternity. The tips of his fingers felt the hard surface of the schooner's rail before he actually saw the vessel. Eager hands reached down to grab him.

Struggling to catch his breath, he looked up into the anxious faces before him. "I think I can take someone on my back. Who'll be the first to come?"

When nobody volunteered, William told them, "You'll all die for certain if you stay here. You might die if you come with me, too, but what's the difference? At least you might have a fighting chance. This schooner can't last much longer, you know, and we're just wasting valuable time here like this."

Still nobody offered, until a tiny woman, who looked to be in her fifties or sixties and probably weighed less than a hundred pounds, spoke up. "I'll come."

Then one of the men spoke for the first time. "No, Aunt Liza, I'll go. Then if you sees that I makes it you might all have more nerve to try it. I don't want to die out here. I'd just as soon take my chances out there in the water anyway."

"Okay," said William, "take off your boots and coat and come on. Just put your arms around my neck, but not too tight or we'll both drown. Just trust me. I'll get you there."

Before leaving, he asked, almost as an afterthought, "Who's in charge here anyway?"

When Albert Rideout, the *Sea Clipper's* captain, acknowledged his position by lifting his hand, William told him, "When I get back have someone else ready to come right away."

With that, William pushed away from the schooner with the arms of the man, who he would later find out was a Joseph Dawe from Cupids, hooked firmly over his shoulders and neck. Surprisingly, the swim to shore, even with the added weight of another person, was no more difficult than his trip out had been. William's powerful breast-strokes were assisted by the waves and tides that pushed both men toward the beach. Before he realized that he was even close to shore, a large wave swept them both onto the beach, and he felt the rocks and the sand beneath his feet.

He was already tired. He needed to rest and catch his breath. His heart thumped wildly in his heaving chest, and his great body was numbed by the icy water. Spread-eagled on the beach, he stayed for forty seconds. Then he ventured out into the water again.

Rideout, true to his word, had another person ready when William reached the schooner for the second time. It was the woman he had heard referred to earlier as Aunt Liza. Without a word, she lowered herself into the water and placed her thin arms around William's neck. As they moved toward shore, she seemed almost weightless on his back. When he surrendered her into the waiting arms of Joseph Dawe on the beach and turned around to swim back out again, William heard her say, "God bless you, my son. I knows He sent you here this day to save a few of us poor sinners."

Later, when they compiled a summary of the men and women that William brought ashore from the ill-fated *Sea Clipper* that day, the woman was listed as Elizabeth Stringer[13] of Grates Cove, aged sixty-three. Having thus survived Spotted Island, she would live another twenty-six years to the age of eighty-nine, outlasting three husbands and able to tell twenty-seven grandchildren and great-grandchildren about her great adventure.

In the first thirty minutes, which seemed like hours to William and the men and women still waiting on the *Sea Clipper*, six people were brought to the safety of the beach. But by then Jackman's great strength was beginning to wane. He desperately wanted to get a few more people off the schooner before he gave out completely. He wondered what was keeping Holwell and the others.

The seventh person was a middle-aged, heavy-set man who continued to cling to the railing of the schooner until William growled at him, "Come on, b'y, or let someone else have yer place." When he finally slipped into the water, the man gripped Jackman's neck so tightly that William had to pry the man's fingers loose and order him to lighten his grip. As they made their way toward shore, William sensed that the man on his back was more frightened than had been any of the other six people he had already carried to the beach. Halfway to shore, a larger than usual wave suddenly lifted both men partially out of the water, tumbling them over before submerging them in its boiling foam. William felt the death-grip of the petrified man's fingers crushing his windpipe, shutting off the air to his lungs. Locked in a deadly embrace, both men sank below the surface. William fought desperately, but the weight of the man whose grip on his throat was choking the life from his body, kept both men plunging further into the depths of the water.

Knowing that he was about to die, William made one last superhuman effort to drive upward, using every ounce of strength that his powerful arms and legs still possessed. When they broke the surface, he looked into the glazed eyes of the crazed man, still clinging wildly to him. He had no other choice. Reaching back as far as possible, he struck the man full in the face with his enormous fist. He felt bone break with the impact, and the sudden gush of blood reddened the water around them for several seconds. He felt the man go limp. Sucking in great gulps of air to refill his starved lungs, William grabbed the now unconscious man by the hair of his head and tried again to make for shore. In the short space of time that had elapsed while the struggle was taking place, the waves and the tide had carried them closer to the beach. Almost unconscious himself, William hardly felt the hands that pulled him and his burden from the water.

He was spent. The struggle had sapped the last ounce of his strength. He needed to rest. He wanted only to sleep. The sweet state of euphoria that swept over him as he sank to the ground obliterated all other thoughts. He lay on the rocky beach, oblivious to everything around him, even the intensely cold air and the waves still breaking over his head and body. He didn't even know that the others had pulled him further up on the beach

He laid there for several minutes. Then, from a great distance he heard a woman's voice telling him, "Don't worry, my son. You done your best. There's not another man alive who could have done what you did today. There's seven of us here on the beach that will be owing to you for the rest of our lives. You're an angel sent by God. Now, my son, you better get your clothes on or you'll freeze to death yourself."

Struggling to open his eyes, the face of the woman that he vaguely remembered carrying ashore earlier gradually came into focus. It showed more compassion than he had ever seen before on the face of any human being. He tried to get up, but couldn't. He was disoriented. It was several moments before the sight of the stranded schooner reminded him of where he was. Then, reaching far down into the depths of his great body, he somehow found a yet-untapped reserve of strength and energy. Rising to his feet, he turned and entered the sea for the eighth time.

But now his body was working on its own. His mind was blank. His powerful arms and legs moved of their own accord. He hardly felt the numbing coldness of the icy water. Time ceased to exist. When he reached the railing of the *Sea Clipper* he didn't even speak. He merely waited until the next person attached himself to his neck and shoulders. Something in the dim recesses of his mind told him to swim for shore.

He was returning from his eleventh trip out to the stranded schooner when John Holwell returned, bringing with him a dozen men from the community. Many others, including most of Jackman's own crew, would arrive soon after as the news of the happenings on the north side of the island spread rapidly through Spotted Island Harbour. Some of the men had dragged a punt with them, but the small boat could not be successfully launched and played no significant part in the events that ensued. Those first to arrive were astounded by what William had done.

By the time Jackman and the man he was bringing ashore with him reached the beach, the Holwell brothers had sprung into action. The coils of rope that they had brought back with them were quickly tied end to end until there was enough continuous rope to span the distance from the shore to the ill-fated schooner. One end was looped around a huge boulder on the beach. Some of the other men were gathering driftwood and kindling to start a fire to warm the eleven survivors who shivered uncontrollably, still unbearably cold, wet, and frightened from their harrowing experience in the water.

John Holwell realized more than anybody else the enormity of the effort that Jackman had already given. He could see it in William's grim expression and the painful, jerky movements of his body. He urged him to rest. When Jackman told him, "I can't stop while there's anyone left out there. I'll drop first".

Holwell replied, "Well, then take a drop of this before you go again."

The dark rum burned like fire in his throat and chest. He felt life returning to his limbs as the fiery liquid coursed through his veins, reviving him a little.

"Give me the rope." With the free end of the coil looped around his waist, William entered the water yet again. Three minutes later he he handed the end of the rope to Captain Rideout, who fastened it securely to the rail of the *Sea Clipper*. They now had a lifeline to the shore. Now, in contrast to his earlier efforts, he could partially swim and pull himself hand over hand along the rope toward the beach while keeping a firm grip on the person that he was helping. The presence of the lifeline also enabled him to get back out to the stranded schooner much easier, thus helping him conserve the last of his rapidly dwindling strength.

He made fourteen more trips. Each time he was met by either John or Samuel Holwell who came part way out on the lifeline to help him take the next survivor the final fifty or sixty feet to the beach. On his final trip, William brought back Skipper Albert Rideout, the last man standing on the stranded schooner. From beginning to end, the rescue operation had taken almost two and a half hours. Miraculously, the *Sea Clipper* still clung tenaciously to the reef. It would be almost another hour before she finally broke up and disappeared into the sea.

As he stumbled onto the beach for the final time, William was surrounded by the crowd. Someone threw a heavy coat over his shoulders. Another man placed his own cap on William's great head. Hardly anyone spoke. There was no backslapping or cheering. The crowd was hushed. Many of the men and women on the beach still couldn't believe the colossal feat of bravery and endurance that they had just witnessed.

Someone thrust a mug of scalding tea into William's hands. As he gulped the steaming liquid, he felt warmth and life returning to his frozen body. He was exhausted, almost asleep on his feet. He suddenly wanted only to be left alone and to feel the comfort and warmth of his own bed.

As he looked around for his clothes, he vaguely heard someone, probably one of the Holwells, say, "Thank God, everybody got off. It's amazing. I never seen anything like it."

It was several seconds before the reply of someone else in the crowd registered in William's brain: "All except for poor Myra. I allow she's dead by now anyway."

Turning to face the man who he thought had spoken the words, William demanded, "Who's Myra? Where is she?"

Someone volunteered the information that Myra Batten[14], the forty-one-year-old-cook of the *Loon*, from Clarke's Beach in Conception Bay, had been severely injured in the earlier collision between the *Loon* and the *Sea Clipper* and was lying, most likely dead, in the cabin of the stranded vessel.

"Why didn't someone tell me before?" William roared.

"Well, it don't matter now. Even if she's still alive, she'd never make it in through the water anyway. Let her 'bide where she is, my son, the Saviour will take care of her now."

"No, by God!" William's great bellow startled the men and women standing before him, "Alive or dead, I can't leave her there."

Then, for the twenty-seventh time, Jackman ventured out again into the raging sea. After the first few strokes, William knew that the short rest on the beach had stripped him of the last of his strength and endurance. He could barely move his arms and legs. They were lead weights. The icy water once again numbed his great body. Shutting his mind to everything except the schooner that lay a couple of hundred yards beyond, he willed himself onward. At one point he wanted to give up and turn back. But the image of Myra Batten lying in the cabin of the *Sea Clipper* would not permit him to stop. Somehow he made it to the rail of the doomed vessel for the last time. He had to rest for several minutes before he gathered enough strength to climb onto the slanting deck and make his way to the forecastle. He did not see the woman until his eyes became accustomed to the darkness below. Then he saw her lying face down by the wall of the forecastle where she had been thrown when the *Sea Clipper* had struck the reef. Only her head and shoulders were above water. He heard her moan softly, but the woman seemed unaware of William's presence.

Cradling the injured woman's thin body as gently as possible in his massive arms, he carried her to the railing where he somehow managed to tie her to his back and shoulders. Her body

*Postage stamp issued in 1992 by Canada Post
to commemorate Jackman's bravery.*

jerked involuntarily when he lowered himself and the woman into the water. For a second or two she opened her eyes and looked wildly about and then slumped back into unconsciousness. Trying to shield her as best he could from the waves that rolled over them continuously, he worked his way hand over hand along the rope until they were close to shore. Then John Holwell and another man took her from his arms and carried her up onto the beach.

Myra Batten would never recover from her injuries. She lived for two more days in the house of Samuel Holwell. She awoke only twice from her deep sleep. In a lucid moment, she asked Judith Holwell to thank the man who had carried her in from the schooner. "I didn't want to die out there all by myself." They were the last words she ever spoke.

William never knew how they got back to Spotted Island Harbour. His first recollection in the aftermath of the rescue was the anxious face of a woman peering searchingly at him when he opened his eyes for the first time in almost twenty-four hours. For a brief moment, he thought it was Bridget and wondered what he was doing back home. Then he realized that it was Madeline Holwell. The dull pain that gripped his entire body told him to go back to sleep again. His eyes burned and his great head felt as if it would burst at any minute. When he tried to sit up in the bed, Madeline stopped him.

"William Jackman, you'll stay there till I tells you you're ready to get up. If you ventures to try it I'll have you tied down to the bed, and you better listen to me or else. I'm going to get you some soup and a drop of tea now . . . and you should try to drink it, cause you haven't had a bite in your body for a long time. You must be starved."

Two days later Jackman rejoined his crew on the *Hawke*. The storm had passed, and the day was bright and clear. Even though twenty-six of the twenty-seven people that William had rescued were safely housed with the families of Spotted Island or were already on their way back home to Conception Bay, many other vessels and their crews were not as fortunate. The great October

Gale of 1867, in its fury, had taken forty-two ships and claimed the lives of forty other men, women and children.

As Jackman boarded the *Hawke*, his crew watched him in reverent silence. They had always loved and respected their captain, but now he was a god. Some of them still couldn't fully fathom the enormous deed he had performed. They hardly knew how to speak to him as his painfully slow steps took him aboard the vessel. Uncharacteristically, it was the eccentric Isaac Barnes who spoke first, "Welcome aboard, Skipper."

Then the other men cheered and came forward one by one to greet their skipper. Within the hour the *Hawke* was on her way. The bulk of Spotted Island gradually disappeared into the distance. William sipped on a mug of steaming tea as he gave instructions for the voyage ahead.

CAPT. WM. JACKMAN'S

Famous Rescue of 27 Lives

At The Spotted Islands in 1867.

(From the Newfoundlander, Nov. 29, 1867.)

The recent hurricane on the coast of Labrador will be long remembered amongst us, not only as the occasion of widespread disaster and mourning, but for some acts of heroism rarely equalled and perhaps never surpassed in the annals of noble daring. One of these, and we believe, the most memorable connected with that dreadful visitation, has been brought under our notice by the following letter from Mr. Matthew Warren to the Right Rev. Dr. Mullock, in relation to the coduct of Captain William Jackman, of this place, in the rescue of no less than seven and twenty lives, which but for his exertion, must inevitably have been sacrificed.

Harbor Grace, Nfld. Nov. 6.

My Lord,—I had intended after my conversation with the Rev. Fathe O'Donnell last week, to call on yo Lordship. On my way to the Pa! you passed, and now I deem it my a to write you, who, I trust, will r known to your and others the hi meritorious, brave and humane duct of Captain William Jackman, so of Captain Thomas Jackman, of S. John's, who during the violent hurri cane of the 9th of October, was th. means through Providence of saving many lives at the imminent risk of his own. He not only denuded himself of all his own clothing in a snowstorm to clothe, poor, perishing women and children, but swam off and rescued many from drowning, who would otherwise have perished. My Lord, his noble conduct is beyond all praise, and may the Almighty God reward him for the same, here and hereafter.

I trust your Lordship will excuse my addressing you, but I cannot allow such brave conduct as his to pass unnoticed. It is my intention D.V. on arrival in England to apply personally to the Royal Humane Society for a gold medal for him, and in which effort I shall hope for your Lordship's assistance.

I have the honor to remain, Your Lordship's most obedient servant,

MATTHEW H. WARREN,
Justice of Peace for Labrador.

To the Rt. Rev. Dr. Mullock, &c., &c.

The hurricane referred to by Mr. Warren was in all its features, in all its incidents of human misery and woe, the most appalling calamity that has ever within memory befallen our seafaring inhabitants on that coast. Aged men who have spent nearly their whole lives at sea, shudder horror stricken when they recall the fury of the elements on that fatal day, and the heart-rending scenes of agony and death of which they were spectators. It is, but a few days since that one of this class who lately arrived here from Labrador expired from no other known cause than the memory of those scenes which day and night haunted his vision. Every efforts of friends failed to dispel them. His only answers to their entreaties were cries and sobs that might have come from a child. He was literally withered and blighted out of life by the pitiless images ever present to his mind of those whom the storm had swept away under his eyes. It was into the midst of such terrors as this killed this poor fellow to think of, that Capt. Jackman rushed, for the accomplishment of deeds which should forever endear him to this, the country of his birth, and which will do honor to our common nature wherever this tale is told. A vessel called the 'Sea Slipper' struck on a reef on the Spotted Islands, Labrador. She had been in collision with another schooner and sank her near Indian Tickle, taking on board her crew and passengers. It was between noon and one o'clock when the 'Sea Skipper' struck the fatal reef, the hurricane blowing at its full from the north-west, and she almost immediately fell asunder, with twenty-seven souls on board. The situation of these poor creatures the reader can imagine, but they were not long left to despair. Captain Jackman came upon the scene as if moved by a special inspiration. He could not account for having strayed there from the shore—he had never seen the spot before, and yet, in his own words, "he felt something telling him to take that course." He saw his work at a glance, and alone and unaided proceeded to do it. Betwen him and the wreck at the nearest point lay over a hundred fathoms of raging sea, and into this he plunged, having first found means of sending to the Spotted Islands for assistance. His power as a swimmer seems hardly less wonderful than the courage that impelled him, and striking out for the wrecked vessel, he conquered even the mad fury of the element and reached on board. Eleven times he swam between the wreck and the shore, each time bringing one man off and placing him in safety. By the time these eleven lives were saved, some men arrived from the Spotted Islands with ropes, and having secured a rope to the shore and around his person, Captain Jackman again dashed off to the rescue of those remaining on the wreck. Making sixteen trips more each way he brought on shore the other sixteen men, the wind and the sea continuing at their utmost violence the whole time. Nor was his work of deliverance yet complete, the crowning triumph was still to come. There was a woman left on board who was believed to be either dead from suffering or so nearly dead that the attempt to move her must be fatal. Living or dead, said Capt. Jackman, when he heard of her, I'll not leave her there, and once again he flung himself amid the waves, and again reached the shore, supporting the frame of this poor exhausted woman. Life was not yet extinct in her, and Capt. Jackman, taking off his flannels, wrapped them around her, and she survived a very short time, only long enough to join her companions in pouring forth her heart's gratitude, and invoking Heaven's benedictions upon their deliverer. Captain Jackman then took the others to the Spotted Islands, where he had all things provided that were necessary for their comfort.

Conduct like this, Mr. Warren truly says, is beyond praise. The best words are weak to express its merit or the degree of admiration which fill every mind that contemplates it. The man whose humanity and courage were equal to such services may well be proud of the soul within him; and yet, it was with difficulty, almost in spite of the reluctant modesty which so commonly accompanies true greatness, that these details have been drawn from him. He seemed when spoken to on the subject, to think of all that he had achieved as of the ischarge of some ordinary duty which claimed no recognition. But not so will it or should it be thought, or spoken of either abroad or at home. We believe and sincerely trust that Mr. Warren's representation to the Humane Society will be fitly responded to; and here in Captain Jackman's own conntry, we also hope he will receive some substantial expression of that feeling which his conduct must universally inspire.

Newspaper clipping of the famous rescue from The Newfoundlander, dated November 29, 1867.

Life After the Rescue

HE DID NOT DREAM OF PRAISE OR FAME
WHEN THE FOAMING SEAS DID RISE,
HE HAD NO THOUGHT THAT HIS DARING DEED
SHOULD BE IMMORTALIZED.

— "The Great Rescue"
P.J. Wakeham

In 1965, Labrador City, in the heart of western Labrador, was still a brand new community barely four years old. Gone were the heady days of early exploration, development, and construction. Just a few miles south of the former mining construction site known as Carol Lake, named for the large fresh water lake upon whose shores it stood, was now a bustling, energetic community. It had its full complement of schools, churches, banks, shopping malls, public buildings, sports and recreational facilities, and amenities of every type.

The influx of people to operate the giant iron ore mine and its supporting infrastructure had come mostly from the island portion of Newfoundland. They brought with them the enthusiasm, drive, and know-how to transform the frontier mining site into a modern town comparable to anything else anywhere in Newfoundland and Labrador.

And now the town was finally getting one of the last essential pieces that would make it a fully functioning, self-supporting community. The Hon. Joseph R. Smallwood and a number of other distinguished guests and dignitaries had been flown in for the official opening of a brand new fifty-bed hospital equipped to handle almost any type of medical emergency. The new facility was built to serve not only the citizens of Labrador City, but also the people of Wabush, another mining town only three miles away, the French town of Fermont on the Quebec side of the border, and anybody else in Labrador who wished to avail of its services. No longer would seriously ill or injured patients have to be flown to St. Anthony, Goose Bay or St. John's.

One of the many committees that had been appointed to oversee and coordinate the different aspects of the hospital's development had been given, among other things, the task of coming up with an appropriate name for the new facility.

The men and women on the committee took their responsibility seriously. They deliberated long and carefully, and met many times on the matter. Their objective was two-fold. Firstly, they wanted to follow in the Newfoundland tradition of naming hospitals, public buildings, bridges, highways, and other structures after men and women who had made a significant contribution to the province at some time or other. Institutions like the Lady Northcott Hospital in Grand Falls, the James Paton Memorial Hospital in Gander, and the large children's hospital in St. John's, named for the famous Dr. Charles Janeway, helped to preserve the names of these individuals in Newfoundland history. Even some of the old cottage hospitals that were now at the end of their useful lives had been named for some deserving individual, like the A. M. Guy Memorial Hospital in Buchans, for the beloved local doctor who had faithfully served the residents of the area for many years.

The second part of the committee's objective was equally important. The members felt it incumbent upon themselves to come up with a name that would in some way be directly related to the Labrador portion of the province.

They invited suggestions from the public. An obvious candidate would have been Sir Wilfred Grenfell. But that name was already taken. The Grenfell Hospital in St. Anthony stood as a living monument to the great English medical missionary who had dedicated most of his life to the health and welfare of the people of northern Newfoundland and Labrador. Another obvious choice was Smallwood, for the province's first premier whose unstinting efforts over a period of many years was finally resulting in the development of the vast natural resources of Labrador that he often said would lead the province into the twenty-first century. But the Smallwood name had already been used for several other important sites.

Other favoured suggestions included commemorating the names of Dr. Harry Paddon and Nurse Myra Bennett. Paddon, a recruit of Grenfell, established clinics, hospital facilities, and schools in coastal Labrador in the early 1900's and dedicated his entire life to serving the settlers and native peoples of Labrador. Bennett, a trained nurse who moved from London, England, to Daniel's Harbour in 1921, spent the best part of her life ministering to the sick and injured people of the Great Northern Peninsula, often under the most adverse conditions imaginable. She travelled the two-hundred-mile stretch of the Peninsula in all sorts of weather by dog team, boat, horse and cart, and in later years, by Bombardier snowmobile. Someone even put forward the name of John C. Doyle, the U.S. tycoon who had masterminded

Captain William Jackman Memorial Hospital in Labrador

another giant mining project in the harsh and hostile interior of Labrador, the nearby Wabush Mines. But by then Doyle's star was already beginning to fade, and the man who would eventually become a fugitive from his own country was an appropriate choice only in the eyes of the person who had made the suggestion.

Through it all, one name kept popping up—Captain William Jackman. Although they kept his name on the list, nobody on the committee seemed to know very much about him. Finally one of the committee members thought that in fairness to all of the suggestions that had been made, he should do some research on this man. He was astounded by what he found out. When he told the others, they too were amazed. Their job was done.

Ironically, but for the efforts and perseverance of one man ninety-eight years earlier, the exploits of Jackman would have most likely long since faded into obscurity, and the plaque being unveiled during the inauguration ceremonies for the new hospital would have borne some other name.

That man was Matthew H. Warren, a Justice of the Peace for Labrador. Most of his time each year was spent in Cartwright, where people from the community and other nearby settlements brought their problems and legal issues to him for resolution. But at least twice a year he made the long trip by boat up and down the coast of Labrador to visit most of the small hamlets and villages where, invariably, some unfinished piece of business awaited his arrival.

It was while he was on one of his semi-annual sojourns that he happened to be on Spotted Island on the day that Jackman had performed his incredible feat of bravery and endurance. He hadn't actually been on the north side of the island where the rescue scene had unfolded, but he was present in Spotted Island Harbour when they brought the survivors back.

Warren was one of the few educated men in Labrador at that time, and, luckily, for the benefit of future Newfoundlanders and Labradorians, he was also a visionary with a keen sense of history. As he listened to the stories told to him by the survivors of the *Sea Clipper* and the *Loon*, and to those of the other people who had witnessed the event, he instinctively knew that this was something that had to be preserved for future generations. So he wrote it all down to record the event for posterity, even though at the time he had no idea what he would eventually do with the information.

In the three days that Warren spent on Spotted Island, he talked to almost all of the survivors and others who had witnessed, and in some cases also participated in, the rescue operation. He even spent a few minutes with Jackman himself. But he got less information from Jackman than from anybody else that he talked with. When Warren asked him what he thought the outcome might have been had he not been present at the scene, Jackman simply replied, "I don't know. I suppose they might have got ashore some other way. That's something that no one will ever know."

Two or three weeks later, Warren transcribed the rough notes that he had taken on Spotted Island into a better organized version of the events that had taken place there. In his own mind, he was still trying to come to grips with the enormity of Jackman's achievement. The details of the rescue were still as vivid in his mind as they were on the day that they had been related to him.

His problem now was that he didn't know how to use the information to ensure that Jackman would be given the recognition that he rightfully deserved in Newfoundland history. Other than the fishing and freighting schooners that came and went between the settlements of Newfoundland and Labrador, there was no other means of communications whereby Jackman's great deed could be made known to the population as a whole. The few newspapers that existed in Newfoundland at the time had small local circulation and, in any case, were not an option for the illiterate majority of the population. He was hesitant to pass his information along to anybody without first knowing for sure that there would be a strong commitment to use it in the best possible manner.

He continued to wrestle with the problem that now obsessed him night and day until he finally hit upon the solution. The best way to reach men and women everywhere, he felt, especially those engaged in the fishing industry, was to tell them Jackman's story from the pulpits of the churches of Newfoundland and Labrador.

With that part of his problem settled in his mind, Warren now gave his undivided attention to determining how Jackman himself might best be recognized and rewarded for his great feat of bravery and endurance. He didn't have to think long to conclude that formal recognition by the Royale Humane Society of London would, if it could be obtained, be the most appropriate way.

Furthermore, being by now so taken with his project that he had to see it through to the end, he decided that he himself, hopefully with the support of a number of high ranking personages from the capital city of St. John's, would make the petition to the Society on Jackman's behalf.

In November, he made the long trip by schooner to St. John's. There he booked a passage on a vessel about to leave for England and made a quick visit to an old acquaintance, now the Reverend Father Michael O'Donnel, whom he asked to intercede for him in seeking an audience with Bishop J.T. Mullock, the leader of the Roman Catholic Church in St. John's at the time.

But the meeting was not to be. Bishop Mullock was busy with other commitments at the

Bishop J.T. Mullock, who spread the word of Jackman's heroic feat through the church, and lent his full support to Matthew Warren's application to the Royal Humane Society for formal recognition of Jackman's amazing feat at Spotted Island.

time, and Warren had a ship to catch. There being not much else he could do in the circumstances, he related the whole story to Father O'Donnel, and wrote the following letter to Bishop Mullock, which he then entrusted into the care of his friend.

My Lord:

I had intended after my conversation with the Rev'd. Father O'Donnel last week to call on your Lordship. On my way to the palace you passed and I now deem it my duty to write you whom I think will make known to your flock and others the highly meritorious, brave and humane conduct of Captain William Jackman, son of Captain Thomas Jackman of St. John's, who during the violent hurricane of October 9, was the means through Providence of saving many lives at the imminent risk of his own. He not only denuded himself of all his clothing in a snow storm to clothe poor perishing women and children, but swam off and rescued many from drowning who would have otherwise perished. My Lord, his noble conduct is beyond all praise and may the Almighty God reward him for the same here and hereafter.

I trust your Lordship will excuse my addressing you, but I cannot allow such conduct as his to pass unnoticed. It is my intention on my arrival in England to appeal personally to the Royal Humane Society for a Gold Medal for him and in which effort I should hope for your Lordship's assistance.

Your Lordship's Most Obedient Servant:
Matthew H. Warren,
Justice of the Peace for Labrador.

The efforts of Warren were rewarded ten months later, in September of the following year, with the arrival of a package at Government House containing a silver medal and a certificate of recognition for Jackman. Accompanying the packet was a letter requesting that they be presented to him on behalf of the Royal Humane Society. The Society had indeed agreed with Warren's assertion that Jackman's great deed epitomized the strength of character, courage, and compassion for his fellow man on which the Society based its awards.

Unfortunately, Jackman was away on the *Hawke* at the time and was not expected back until late October or early November. This, however, gave Governor Anthony Musgrave ample time to plan a reception fitting for the hero whose exploits were by now beginning to spread rapidly throughout Newfoundland and Labrador.

The reception wasn't something that Jackman looked forward to. His brother Arthur simply laughed when William suggested that he fill in for him and accept the awards on his behalf. He tried his father, Thomas, too, who bluntly told him, "No, go and get it yourself."

Governor Musgrave, with the extra time, had indeed organized a reception worthy of the occasion. Among the invited guests were the members of Jackman's own family, the Bowrings (John, Edward and Henry), a number of politicians of the day, newspapers, and many others. Also among the elite who attended was Bishop Mullock, who, as Matthew Warren had requested, had indeed told Jackman's story to his flock. He had gone a step further and written a strong letter of recommendation to the Royal Humane Society in London endorsing Warren's petition. With a touch for the dramatic, the Governor had also invited a well known local poet of the time, Marcus Hopkins, who opened the reception with a poem that he had composed for the occasion.

Jackman, The Hero

ATTENTION all both great and small, and harken to this tale
Of eighteen hundred sixty-seven and the great "October Gale,"
A gale that lashed the Labrador, and brought undying fame
To a modest Newfoundlander, William Jackman was his name.

In early June he had left Renews down on the Southern Shore,
And sailed to Spotted Island on the coast of Labrador,
The fishery fair; the season long; now plans were under way
To head back home to Newfoundland without too much delay.

On the morning of October ninth the dawning sky forebode,
A storm was in the offing; the dazzling sun-hounds showed;
So extra lines and anchors to his schooner were made fast,
As Captain Jackman waited for the onslaught of the blast.

The wind came up with driving sleet and veered to the northeast,
The Atlantic breakers rolled ashore, their crests a frothy yeast,
As equinoctial fury shrieked out in hideous glee
Its portent of disaster wrought by the tireless sea.

Meanwhile Jackman's schooner, on the island's leeward side,
Was riding like a breasting gull, secure from wind and tide;
The captain and crew, who for safety's sake were on the beach ashore,
Suddenly heard the sound of guns above the tempest roar.

Quickly Jackman and his men ran to a nearby hill,
And there they saw the dreaded sight which made their blood turn chill,
Two hundred yards or so from shore a craft had come to grief,
And in the wild and seething sea was foundering on a reef.

The Sea Clipper was the schooner, and she had sailed that day,
Hoping to reach before the storm the shelter of Table Bay;
With twenty-seven souls on board, her boats swept from her deck,
There she lay on the jagged reef, a broken, helpless wreck.

Back for ropes went Jackman's crew as quickly as could be,
While Jackman doffing coat and boots plunged in the foaming sea;
With sturdy strokes and spirit brave he reached the doomed craft's rail,
And with one of the crew upon his back turned shoreward without fail.

Back and forth, and forth and back, he swam the raging sea,
No fewer than twenty-six lives he saved from awful tragedy;
Still one remained, a woman frail, dying or perchance dead,
"The risk's too great, 'tis only madness to go again," they said.

Jackman replied, "Living or dead, out there she'll not remain,"
So with a rope around his waist, he started out again.
At last with anxious eyes they saw him swimming to the shore,
And slowly but surely to the land her dying form he bore.

Yet none too soon, for not long thence with a resounding roar,
The Sea Clipper was rent in twain, and then was seen no more;
And on their knees in grateful prayer they gave thanks for him so brave,
Who spared not himself to save them all from a certain watery grave.

Many are the sagas about men who go down to the sea,
Of superhuman strength and feats and deeds of bravery,
But the name of William Jackman forevermore will stand
Among the immortal heroes in the annals of Newfoundland.

At the end of Hopkins' recital, Thomas Jackman turned to some of the people near him and spoke of his son. "You know, if William didn't go back for that woman, I think I'd disown him." It was the only public comment he was ever heard to make on the matter,

The Governor, taking full advantage of the occasion, as any astute politician would, made a long and glowing speech, at the end of which he read out for the audience the words on Jackman's certificate of recognition.

Jackman, obviously uncomfortable with the whole proceeding, received his silver medal and certificate of recognition[15] and gave a brief speech to the audience. A few minutes later, in a moment when everyone's attention was focused on another speaker, Jackman passed his diploma and medal to his wife and said,

"Bridget, put these away somewhere for me." He never again, after that night, voluntarily showed either item to anyone. As the years passed, however, he sometimes retrieved them from the bureau drawer in which they were kept and looked at them in the privacy of his own bedroom. When he did so, the events of Spotted Island were still as fresh in his mind as they were on the day that they occurred.

Having survived the reception, Jackman went back to his work. Word of his exploits had by now spread throughout the

Royal Humane Society
Instituted 1774

for the recovery of persons apparently Drowned or Dead

PATRON
Her Majesty the Queen

VICE PATRON
H.R.H. The Duke of Argyll, K.T.

Court holden at the Society's Office Trafalgar Square
Wednesday the 2nd day of July
Sir Walter Stirling Burl in the Chair

It was resolved unanimously
That the noble courage and humanity displayed by
Captain William Jackman

in having on the 9th October 1867 repeatedly plunged in the sea during a hurricane to the relief of the passengers and crew of the schooner the Sea Slipper wrecked at Spotted Island, Labrador, and saved the lives of twenty-seven persons, calls forth the admiration of this General's Court and justly entitles him to the Honorary Silver Medal of this Society which is hereby presented to him.

Laublon Young   **Argyll**

———   ———

Secretary   *President*
                                                     Chairman

island and along the coast of Labrador. For years afterward, whenever the *Hawke* steamed into some village or settlement, people always came to get a glimpse of Jackman, the Hero. They wanted to be able to tell their children and grandchildren that they had shaken the hand of this great man.

The ever humble and unassuming Jackman did not take well to his newfound fame, and the passage of time did little to lessen his desire for privacy. It was always a relief to him when they entered some community that was either unaware of the *Hawke's* coming or had not yet heard about Jackman's heroic actions at Spotted Island. Invariably, however, before he left again, the story would somehow leak out. Although they denied it, Jackman always suspected that his crew was responsible. Then news of his presence in the community would spread like wildfire, and his hoped-for peace and privacy would be lost for the remainder of the visit.

Because of his work, in 1869 Jackman moved his family to St. John's where they lived in a two-storey frame house on Brine Street, one of a block of four houses that his father had purchased a few years earlier. Although it was two years since his Spotted Island heroics, he was still besieged by well-wishers and curiosity-seekers wherever he went. Bridget tried to shield him from the publicity that she knew he disliked, but his children, so proud of their courageous father, took advantage of every possible occasion to tell his story. They themselves basked in the fame of their heroic parent and enjoyed the attention and special status that fell their way when they told his story.

Jackman and the *Hawke*, and later the *Eagle*, made many more voyages together. He still looked forward to the long trips up the Labrador coast, taking the same delight in the sights and the people of Labrador as he had on that first occasion many years ago. He always tried to find time to stop in at Spotted Island for a visit, sometimes staying overnight with one of the Howell brothers. Ironically, he never again visited the small cove on the northern side of the island where the rescue had taken place. Every time the *Hawke* steamed past Indian Harbour, he also thought about

Aunt Maggie. At times he seemed to think that he even felt her presence again.

In 1871, Jackman's great popularity was the drawing card that Father Daniel Lynch needed to found the Star of the Sea Association in St. John's. The Protestant equivalent, the Society of United Fishermen (S.U.F.), had been founded by the Rev. George Gardner, a Church of England minister in Heart's Content, a few years earlier. With Jackman as its first president and main attraction, enrolment in the new Star of the Sea Association quickly grew to 1,500 in the first three months of its existence, making it the largest association of its kind at the time. Within the space of a few short years, fellow associations sprang up all across the island. The association, whose stated goal was to provide mutual benefits and social activities for its members, was restricted to Roman Catholics. It would be almost a hundred years before the association opened its doors to men of all denominations. By then its focus, too, had changed to one of community enrichment, and the sponsorship of sporting events and other community activities.

An outspoken and energetic Roman Catholic priest, Father Lynch's genuine heartfelt sympathy for the plight of Newfoundland's poor fishermen had spurred him to a life of service dedicated to their cause. His initial instinct had been to try to create a collective of fishermen who, in large enough numbers, might be able to pressure the fishing merchants of St. John's and the other large fishing centres of Newfoundland into improving the lot of the continually downtrodden fishermen. At a time when most Newfoundland fishermen lived in constant poverty, the fishing and sealing merchants continued to amass incredible wealth while remaining oblivious to the hardship and hunger of the thousands of men who were the very underpinning of their wealthy empires. The initial reaction of the fishermen to Father Lynch's attempts to start such an initiative, however, quickly convinced him of the futility of his efforts. Surprised by the resistance he met, but understanding it nevertheless, he revised the mandate of his envisioned association in a manner that he knew would still benefit the fishermen he so loved and admired. It wasn't until

William Coaker came along in 1908 that the first successful initiative toward the unionization of Newfoundland's poor fishermen would meet with some success through the establishment of the Fishermen's Protective Union (FPU). Another 50 years would pass before the efforts of Father Desmond McGrath, another enlightened Roman Catholic priest, would see the creation of the Newfoundland Fishermen, Food and Allied Workers Union (NFFAWU).

Shortly after he had helped to found the Star of the Sea Association, Jackman realized for the first time that he didn't seem to have quite the same strength and energy that he had always known. Long accustomed to rising from his bed at 5:00 a.m. or earlier, he now occasionally found himself trying to steal a few extra minutes in the morning. Sometimes he stayed as late as six o'clock or even a little longer.

As the vessel's captain, he was always on deck when there was work to be done or whenever the *Hawke* or the *Eagle* was steaming through rough water or bad weather. But often, when there was a lull in activity, he would retire to his cabin to read or to write in the small diary that he had started a couple of years previously, or simply to rest, handing the operation of the steamer over to the second hand for a few hours.

At the age of thirty-eight, he started to lose weight despite the fact that his appetite was as hearty as ever. Bridget was worried about him. She was especially concerned when one morning, during a short stay at home, Jackman did not get out of bed until nearly 10:00 a.m. More ashamed than alarmed, but still tired and listless, Jackman forced himself to make the twenty-minute walk down to the harbour-front where the *Eagle* lay at anchor. There he chatted for awhile with the two crew members he had left onboard to safeguard the steamer. He found the short walk back home very tiring, and by eight o'clock that evening he was again ready for bed.

The next day, however, he felt much better and was up and about before 5:30 a.m.. He seemed to have recovered much of his old energy and went about his work in the normal vigorous manner. Then, a couple of weeks later, he experienced another similar episode of tiredness.

Over the next two or three months, he made a couple of visits to a doctor, mostly to placate Bridget, who was by now extremely worried about him. On both occasions, the doctor gave Jackman the same diagnosis, "I can't find much wrong with you, Captain Jackman. You're getting on towards forty, you know. Perhaps all those years on the water and the ice are finally taking their toll. I'm going to give you a tonic that should help. If things get any worse come back and see me again."

Despite the doctor's pronouncement of good health, Jackman's periodic bouts of tiredness and weakness intensified and occurred with increasing regularity over the next twelve months. In between what he called his "spells," he occasionally felt like his old self. Still, for the most part he himself realized that his health was failing rapidly. Despite Bridget's constant pleadings, he refused to see the doctor again.

As 1877 neared, Jackman's health degenerated even more rapidly. People who hadn't seen him for awhile were shocked at his gaunt and angular appearance. His once powerful body was now wasted and bent, and his movements were slow and obviously painful. Early in the following February, as the sealing vessels were once again preparing for the annual seal hunt, Jackman took to his bed for the last time. Suddenly too weak to stand alone or to even sit upright in a chair for any length of time, both he and Bridget knew that the end was near.

Concerned as always about his family, Jackman gave instructions and directions from his bed for the execution of his estate and the welfare of his wife and children when he was gone. Even on his deathbed, however, he maintained his keen sense of humour. When Bridget came home with the new suit of clothes in which he would be buried, Jackman teased her gently, saying, "Bridget, girl, now what would I be doing with a good suit like that? Sure it would be better if you gave it to poor ol' Billy Murphy. At least he'd get a bit of wear out of it." He was referring to one of the many "characters" that frequented the streets of St. John's at that time.

Jackman lingered on for eleven days. He occasionally took a little food and warm tea, but most of the time he slept, drifting in and out of consciousness as the days and nights slowly passed. He was often unaware of the flood of friends and relatives that visited his house on Brine Street. Then, in the early morning hours of February 25, 1877, Jackman, the Hero, passed away at the age of thirty-nine.

No one knew for sure what had caused his death. Some said that his heart had given out, while others were of the view that he had died of the silent, creeping disease that we know today as cancer. The most commonly held belief, however, was that his exertions on that terrible October day, nine and a half years earlier, had taken a far greater toll on his powerful body than anyone had realized. They believed that the slow deterioration that eventually killed him had, in fact, started on that very day.

He was laid to rest in Belvedere Cemetery in St. John's on February 28. In tribute to the man whose exploits were unprecedented in the history of Newfoundland and Labrador, the businesses of the capital city closed their doors for the day, and the flags of the city flew at half-mast.

"God Loveth A Cheerful Giver"
Final resting place of Capt. William Jackman and his wife, Bridget,
in Belvedere Cemetery, St. John's.

Captain William Jackman circa 1860

The Jackmans of Renews

(Shipwrecked off Renews in 1637)
William Jackman & Wife Johanna

(Three Generations Later)
Arthur Jackman (b. 1750) & Wife Catherine

(Seven Sons)

Tobias (1781)	Michael (1792)
James (1783)	George (1796)
Thomas (1786)	Arthur (1800)
Philip (1789)	

Thomas Jackman (b. 1808) & Wife Catherine

— **William (b. 1837,
married Bridget Burbridge)**

— James
— Michael
— Arthur
— Johanna
— Lawrence
— Mary

— Samuel
— **William Henry**
— **Frances Mary**
— **Thomas**
— **James**
— **Mary Monica**

The Jackman home in Renews. The family standing in front of the house is that of a Mr. Peter McCarthy, who purchased the house from Thomas Jackman. The house was destroyed by fire in 1909.

Bridget Jackman, William's wife, with their daughter, Monica.

Samuel and James Jackman, sons of
William and Bridget,
in front of the Jackman property
on Brine Street.

James and Thomas Jackman (rear),
sons of
William and Bridget, and
William Jackman, Jr. (grandson).

James Jackman,
William Jackman, Jr.,
Mary (wife of Thomas Jackman),
children Conception, Mary,
Magdeline (daughters of
Thomas Jackman).

Rev. William H. Jackman, son of
William & Bridget, with his step-
grandmother, Sister Monica
(second wife of Thomas).

Mrs. Mona Kennedy,
granddaughter of
Captain William Jackman;
his oldest surviving relative.

Brian Jackman, local
businessman, and
his wife Gio. Brian has
dedicated much of his life
to preserving the history of his
courageous great-grandfather
and the rich tradition of the
Jackmans of Renews.

Epilogue

William Jackman was survived by his wife Bridget and their six children, his brothers Michael, James, and Arthur, and sisters Johanna and Mary. His father, Thomas Jackman, died in 1870 at the age of 62, four years after the passing of his wife, Catherine. "Viking Arthur," the famous sealing captain, whaler and explorer lived to the age of 64. His entire life reads like one long adventure story, but at the end of it all, his greatest claim was that he had taken over eight thousand men out to sea and to the ice, and brought every single one of them safely home again. An interesting footnote in the Jackman story is that Thomas Jackman's second wife, a Monica Walsh from Wexford, Ireland, whom he met in St. John's two years after Catherine's death, joined St. Patrick's Convent in St. John's when Thomas died. There she spent the rest of her days as Sister Monica.

The role of the Holwell brothers, John and Samuel, also did not go unrewarded. In September of 1868, they too were recognized by the Royal Humane Society and were presented with bronze medals for their part in the rescue on Spotted Island. Spotted Island itself, like many other remote Newfoundland and Labrador communities, was included in the resettlement program of the Liberal Government in the early 1960's, and by 1970 the last permanent resident had left the island.

In the summer of 1999, the Captain William Jackman Museum opened its doors for the first time in Jackman's hometown of Renews. The small museum is crammed with artifacts and information about Jackman, and other people and events that occurred in the community and the surrounding area.

Fittingly, the museum is located in the school (no longer in operation) a couple of hundred yards up the hill from the house where Jackman lived as a boy. Only an old set of concrete steps now marks the spot where the Jackman house once stood. A short distance away is the beach and the salt water where Jackman played with the other children of the community, and where he developed the great swimming ability that would eventually make him one of the greatest heroes that Newfoundland and Labrador has ever seen.

The history of Newfoundland and Labrador is filled with innumerable sea rescues in which brave men and women exposed themselves to grave danger to save the lives of others in distress. In 1942, two American destroyers, the *Pollux* and the *Truxtun* went aground in the treacherous waters of Chambers Cove on the Burin Peninsula during extremely rough weather. The men of St. Lawrence and Lawn scaled the steep cliffs to save the lives of one hundred eighty-six of the vessels' crews. Although one hundred ninety-three others were lost, the death toll would have been far greater but for the courage and perseverance of the men from the two small Burin Peninsula communities. As well, the women of St. Lawrence took care of the rescued seamen and nursed many of them back to health before they were eventually returned to their homes in the United States. In 1954, in gratitude to the men and women of St. Lawrence and Lawn for their great humanitarian efforts, the U.S. Government presented the area with a well-equipped hospital which served the people of the Burin Peninsula for many years until its recent closure.

In 1832, a hundred and ten years before the *Pollux* and *Truxtun* disaster, the Harvey family of Isle Aux Morts participated in one of the most amazing rescues ever recorded on the south coast of Newfoundland. From their island home a few miles off Port aux Basques, they saw the distress signal of the *Despatch* which had been blown onto the rocks some distance away by a strong gale. George Harvey, along with his twelve-year-old son and his seventeen-year-old daughter Ann, who would eventually be called the "Grace Darling[16] of Newfoundland," and their Newfoundland dog, Tray, ventured out in the turbulent sea in their small boat to try to save the people on the stranded ship. It took the combined strength of all three of them to row the three miles to the stricken *Despatch*. When they got as close as they possibly could without being dashed to pieces against its side, they threw their Newfoundland dog into the water to swim the rest of the way to the ship. The dog swam back to the Harveys' small boat a few minutes later with a rope around his neck, which the family then towed ashore and fastened to a large boulder on the beach. Using this lifeline, every one of the one hundred sixty-three people on the *Despatch* made it safely to shore. The bravery and daring of George Harvey, and his son and daughter, eventually reached the ears of King William IV of England who rewarded them with a medal and a sack of gold coins. Incredibly, six years later, in almost identical circumstances, the Harvey family saved the lives of another twenty-five people when the Scottish ship, the *Rankin*, went aground in the same area.

Another heroic rescue occurred in late November, 1875, when the schooner, the *Waterwitch*, was driven into the cliffs near Pouch Cove during a wind and rainstorm with twenty hands on board. Nine men were lost, but the eleven others were saved by the valiant efforts of a Pouch Cove fisherman named Alfred Moores. He had himself lowered down over the slippery cliffs to pluck the survivors one by one from the doomed schooner. For his great act of bravery, he was awarded a silver medal and a certificate of recognition by the Royal Humane Society.

These are but a few of the hundreds of epic rescues that have taken place along the coast of Newfoundland and Labrador during the past five hundred years. The men and women who participated in these and other great rescue operations will be forever remembered for their courage and daring, and for the great compassion that they had for their fellow man. Many paid the ultimate price of their own lives in trying to save others. Their courageous actions epitomize the strength and character of Newfoundlanders and Labradorians who have braved the hostile waters of the North Atlantic since the sixteenth century.

Their numbers are many, and their exploits great. But one man among them stands out like a giant. His bravery, strength, and endurance is unsurpassed in the annals of Newfoundland and Labrador. In almost single-handedly saving the lives of twenty-seven men and women under the most overwhelming weather conditions imaginable, he secured for himself forever the unrivaled title of *Jackman, the Hero.*

Medal awarded to William Jackman by the Royal Humane Society of London.

Notes

1 Most accounts of Jackman's exploits refer to this schooner as the *Sea Clipper*. Others including the certificate awarded to him for his courage and bravery by the Royal Humane Society of London, call her the *Sea Slipper*. It is generally believed that *Sea Clipper* is the schooner's correct name.

2 This is not the correct name of this schooner. None of the reference material that I used regarding the Spotted Island rescue operation referred to the vessel by name. The name I have used for her captain is also fictitious.

3 A very thin person, usually a woman or child.

4 A sturdy boat resembling a scaled-down, but stouter, schooner used for fishing or carrying fish. Usually twenty-five to thirty-five feet in length, they had a capacity for about 30 quintals of fish.

5 The act of jumping from one small ice-pan to another, usually following a leader.

6 A game of tag in which a person could not be tagged if he or she cried "goolos" first.

7 Low-lying berry bushes.

8 The name given by the Norse saga to the native people that the Vikings met and fought in their attempt to establish a permanent settlement in Northern Newfoundland.

9   Believed to be the winter settlement of Leif Erickson. L'Anse aux Meadows, on the tip of the Northern Peninsula of Newfoundland, is the first authenticated Norse site in North America.

10   The term for permanent settlers of coastal Newfoundland and Labrador to differentiate them from migratory summer fishermen.

11   Boiled dumplings made with flour, water and raisins or dried figs.

12   The term for migratory fishermen who came to live temporarily in the settlements of northern Newfoundland and Labrador or made their own summer encampments to fish during the summer, differentiating them from the permanent settlers who lived there year round and the migratory "floaters" who lived on and fished from their schooners.

13   A fictitious character.

14   This is not the woman's real name. None of the reference material used for this book referred to her by name.

15   Initially, for some unknown reason, Thomas Jackman was named as the recipient of the certificate. When the error was discovered, it was corrected by simply crossing out Thomas' name and writing in William's.

16   Grace Darling was a young English girl who gained fame by rescuing many people along the coast of Northumberland.

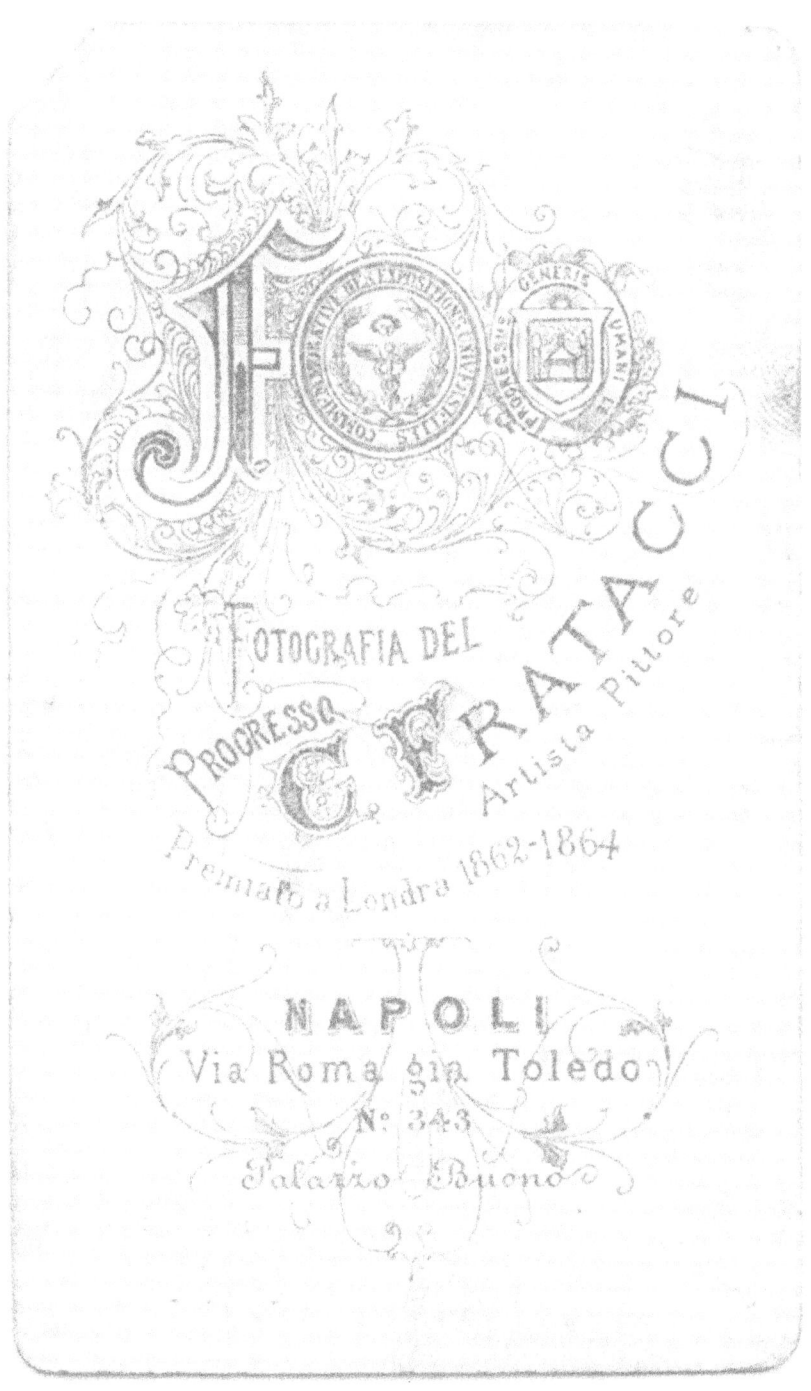

Captain William Jackman's Passport.

Eldon Drodge

About the Author

ELDON DRODGE, born and raised in Newfoundland, recently retired after a thirty-five year career in the computer industry. He now resides with his wife, Joan, in Torbay where gardening, painting, and woodworking are among his many hobbies. A long-standing sports enthusiast, he still plays old-timers' hockey and spends countless hours at the rinks and soccer fields watching his grandsons play.

The many boyhood holidays spent at his birthplace of Little Heart's Ease, Trinity Bay, where he listened to endless stories told by his grandparents, aunts and uncles, instilled in him a deep love of outport life and a lasting interest in the history of his forefathers.

Jackman is his first publication.